The Call of the Raven

Books by Glyn Frewer

THE CALL OF THE RAVEN

GLYN FREWER

Illustrated by
George Woodford

LUTTERWORTH PRESS
CAMBRIDGE

To Lorna, with love

Lutterworth Press
7 All Saints' Passage
Cambridge CB2 3LS

British Library Cataloguing in Publication Data
Frewer, Glyn
The Call of the Raven
I. Title   II. Woodford, George
823'.914 [J]   PZ7
ISBN 0-7188-2669-8

Typeset by Vision Typesetting, Manchester

Printed in Great Britain by
St Edmundsbury Press, Bury St Edmunds, Suffolk

RAVEN (*Corvus corax*)

Class: *Aves*
Order: *Passeriformes*
Family: *Corvidae*
Genus: *Corvus*

There is, I think, no class of birds which, in view of
their high physical and mental development, of their
powers of imitation, of their drolleries and their
delicious aptitude, when domesticated, for fun and
mischief, of their influence through all the earlier
centuries and civilisations – an influence which has not
gone by, even now and here – over the thoughts, the
hopes and the fears of man, is equal in interest to the
crow or corvine tribe. At the head of them all stands
the raven.

R. Bosworth Smith

No wonder that so knowing a bird, gifted, at the same
time, with a voice so deep and solemn as to command
attention wherever it is heard, should, in all ages, have
impressed superstitious people with a notion that it had
something unearthly in its nature.

Edward Stanley

GLOSSARY

afon	river
bran	crow
bronwen	weasel
bwlch	mountain pass
caer, car	fort
cigfran	raven
ddu	black
dinas	castle
esgair	ridge
fan	head of valley
ffwlbart	polecat
foel	hill
goch	red
llyn	lake
maen	stone
nant	stream
pont	bridge

CONTENTS

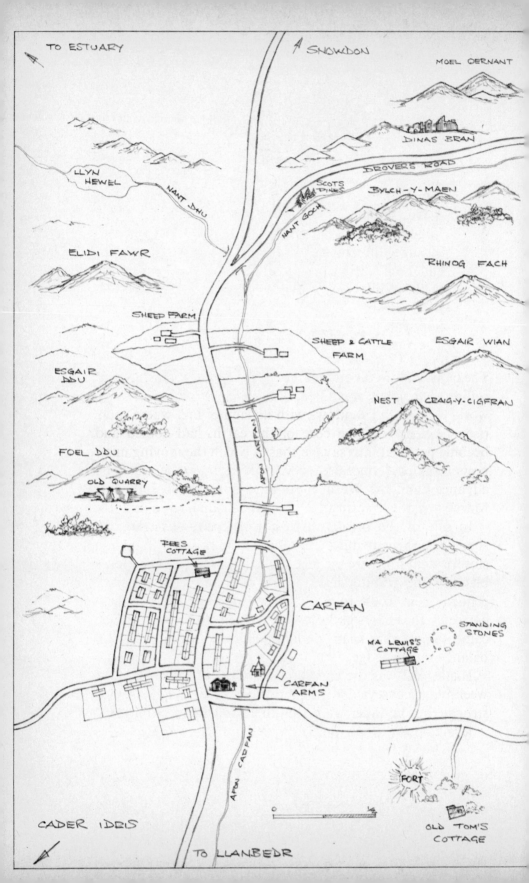

1. Raven's Crag

The cloud billowed between the crags like a sea, cresting and rolling. The valley was filled, obliterated. It was a primeval world of fogs and shadows with no sign of life, where rock, risen molten from the core of the earth, had cooled and become petrified into savage shapes which the moving mists now revealed, concealed, revealed. But as the morning advanced and the Welsh mountains felt the touch of pale March sun, the lowering waves of cloud calmed and thinned.

In one of the breaks, high above Craig-y-Cigfran, the shape of a ragged-edged leaf hung in the sky, spiralling in a slow descent to where the mist drifted like lace. The shape, as black as the granite sheen, rolled over and a harsh croak echoed from rock to rock as a single strong wingbeat corrected the roll. A glide, a second croak and Kra the raven came to rest, his heavy bulk finding an instant, graceful balance on the ledge.

His arrival was the signal for a chorus of calls. The four week-old chicks vied with each other in stridency as they struggled to be taller, shivering their down-covered arms.

Kra hopped along the ledge and up on to the massive

mound of twigs. For nine years, he and Vara, his mate, had reared their broods here, and each year more twigs had been added to the ancient nest they had found when they arrived. Kra stretched out his neck and with a bobbing motion he regurgitated the food from his fully-laden throat-pouch, passing it in his beak to the open mouths of his young. His huge bill, so often a formidable weapon, placed the food into the gaping maws of the chicks with delicate finesse. Eventually, his pouch was empty. The chicks subsided resentfully into silence, though each time Kra moved, a beak would open hopefully.

Kra gazed out through the mist, which was fast disappearing. The jagged edge of Foel Ddu stood less than a mile away, on the opposite side of the valley. For more than twenty years he had reared young on the side of Foel Ddu, before the quarry blasting had bitten into the mountain so that his nest-site was threatened. He and Vara had abandoned it just in time, for the following spring their nesting place, along with two thousand tons of Foel Ddu, had crumpled and slid into the valley where the giant slabs provided many men with many months of labour, splitting them into slates.

The two birds had crossed the valley to the mountain opposite where there were no men and no workings and where the ledge was a perfect natural nesting site. It topped an overhang seventy metres above the scree and was beyond the reach of all but marauding crows, gulls and jackdaws. Above the overhang, the rock bulged, providing cover, and the mountain rose almost sheer for another three hundred metres to a crown of jagged peaks. Though no ravens had nested on it within living memory of the people of the valley, the name itself, Craig-y-Cigfran, which means Raven's Crag, showed it had been used by ravens since time immemorial. The huge mound of rotting branches, twigs and moss was further evidence that Kra had returned to the place of his ancestors.

2

While Kra had nested on Foel Ddu, a pair of peregrines had used the site. After a short winter absence, they had returned to find Kra and Vara in possession, the nest already filled by a brood of half-fledged young. The aggression of the parent ravens had proved too much for the hawks and within a few days they had left the valley.

The mist was finally clearing now as Kra stood motionless on the ledge, ignoring the raucous pleas of the nestlings. Suddenly, his wings opened and he lifted off, soaring out above the valley. His eye, as keen as any peregrine's or buzzard's, had identified the distant black speck as his mate. His deep *korronk, korronk* was answered by her as they closed towards each other.

Her pouch was full and as he passed, Kra closed his wings, rolled over and corkscrewed before setting off with powerful wingbeats to scour the valley fields.

For the next three weeks the ravens spent the daylight hours relaying food to the insatiable nestlings. The young birds grew rapidly and stubbly brown feathers replaced the down, while the ungainly appearance created by their large heads and heavy bills diminished as their bodies filled out. One of the chicks, more venturesome than the rest, learned to clamber up to the edge of the nest and so become the first to be fed. This was Corax, and he soon became the biggest of the brood.

Before long, the other three fledgelings managed to do the same, but by that time Corax had left the nest, tumble-fluttering down to land sprawling on the ledge below. There, amid the accumulated dust and dirt of centuries, he squatted, calling loudly and, once again, was always fed first. A day later, the other young birds joined him and soon all four were fluttering and clambering from the nest at will.

When he was five weeks old, Corax learned to stretch his wings and flap them. They were not yet strong enough to lift

3

him high, but he was able to feel the support they gave his body on each downstroke. This exercise, and eating everything that came his way, was now his daily occupation and he grew rapidly in size and confidence.

The warm April days of soft rain suddenly ended. The wind changed direction, sweeping down the valley from the northeast and all the while increasing. Corax, further from the nest than the other birds, was testing his wings, lifting himself and dropping, rising and falling. The wind gusted and he rose higher than expected and the second gust took him out from the ledge before he could fold his wings. He missed the ledge on the descent and now there was nothing below him but the sheer drop to the scree-clad slope below.

A day or two earlier and Corax would have died. But his wings had gained strength and though the air drove through his slender feathers, his frantic wingbeats provided enough resistance to slow down his rate of descent. In the lee of the mountain, the wind blew less strongly and he was able to give himself direction. Screeching with terror, his strength almost given out, Corax managed to make a heavy, awkward landing on the loose granite scree. He lay, wings extended, as though dead. Then his dove-grey eyes blinked and he pulled his wings in to his side. Now he crouched, panting, beak half-open, and waited for his strength to return.

Kra had seen it all. He had been high above Craig-y-Cigfran and he dropped at once, plummeting with closed wings to level out at the last moment above the helpless fledgeling's head, and coasted to a nearby rock. Seconds later, Vara joined him and their combined, high-pitched anxious calls seemed to revive Corax, for he raised his head and answered feebly.

The two adults hopped nearer to him and Corax staggered to his feet. There was blood on his breast where the sharp stones had cut him and his wings were bruised but he had no

4

serious wounds. He called again and Kra approached him. With his great beak, the adult raven gently preened the straggly displaced feathers on the young bird's wings. Corax mewed softly. Vara, too, moved in to help with the preening.

An hour later, Corax was fed. Kra spiralled down, his throat-pouch full, and Corax ate far more than he would have done had he been obliged to share with the three other fledgelings. And when Kra left, with no more food to give, Vara descended and Corax was fed again.

By nightfall he had eaten more than he had ever had in one day. He hopped clumsily across the stony slope and found a niche between two large rocks where he felt more protected. The wind, which had abated slightly, now brought with it rain and sleet. As the night closed in and Corax began to shiver, missing the warmth of his fellow nestlings, there was a deep croak from nearby. Kra's huge form appeared before the niche and sidled in beside him. There the adult raven stayed, imparting warmth to his offspring for the rest of the night.

The sleet persisted throughout the next day. But Corax was fed by both parents and again he ate more than the others in the nest. Well fed though he was, he never ceased calling for more, and this brought a new danger.

It was evening and darkness was rapidly filling the valley. A russet shape ascended the slope from the fields, moving from rock to rock in a sinewy gliding motion. Erim the stoat had been watching the regular descent of the adult ravens all day and now the light was thickening he ventured nearer until he could hear the persistent calls of the fledgeling. Waiting until Kra had lifted off into driving sleet, he insinuated himself among the stones and approached the unsuspecting bird. He was only ten metres away when Corax saw him.

The young raven froze, his eye on the rock behind which

5

the stoat was crouching. From there, it darted to a nearer one. Corax began to call: shrill, harsh calls of fear. And he began to run, flapping his wings as he went so that his progress was achieved by a succession of long airborne hops. But the lithe shape of Erim the hunter broke from cover and rapidly gained on the bird.

Corax had covered about twenty metres before the stoat was upon him. As the animal leapt, Corax jumped, squawking shrilly, fluttering up out of reach. The stoat whipped round, curled like a spring and leapt again as Corax flapped to the ground.

His front paws landed on an outstretched leg. There was a gentle crack as the bone snapped. The stoat aimed his teeth at the throat, ducking to avoid the beak. But Corax had not the wits to use his most formidable weapon. Squawking and fluttering was his only defence. The sharp teeth plucked his downy plumage as, with frenzied fluttering, Corax tore free at the last moment. But his strength was ebbing and he would not be able to repeat the leap.

The only warning for Erim was a shadow. The stoat reacted instantly, twisting his head upwards and baring his teeth, but he was not quick enough to save himself. The giant shape of the plummeting raven thudded on to him, the claws gripping him like those of a buzzard, and the great bill stabbed once, splitting the stoat's skull into fragments. With a savage, tearing motion, Kra then sheared the head from the body.

Corax kept up his cries, even with the twitching corpse beside him. He ceased only when Kra hopped up to him and preened his head, *pruk, pruking* quietly. Corax was bleeding from a ring of bites in his breast but the wounds were not deep. It was his broken leg that pained him. With difficulty, he hopped on one leg to the cover of a large rock where he crouched, trembling with exhaustion. Kra stood beside him and gradually the shaking ceased. His fear subsided and soon Corax began preening the blood-flecks from his breast feathers. When that was done, he turned towards the adult raven and called for food.

Kra gave a loud *korronk* and lifted off just as Vara descended with a bulging food-pouch. When she had fed Corax, she hopped across to the body of the stoat, tore it into shreds and devoured it. Then she returned to Corax, sidling into the sheltered hollow below the boulder to crouch beside him. Although her warmth protected him, Corax found it impossible to settle comfortably. His injured leg, which was less painful when he held it up, was already showing signs of stiffening.

2. A New Home

"That boy's going to be the death of me."

Mrs Rees eyed her husband tearfully. Emlyn Rees shrugged his narrow shoulders. It was all too much for him. He had troubles of his own at the Water Board. His son's misdemeanours took second place to the worry of possibly losing his job as chief clerk.

"What more can I do, Gwen? He's at a good school. We have a good home for him here. We have the television now. I don't know what gets into him."

His wife sniffed. "A good belting, that's what the boy needs. A good thrashing from a hard man, not a few timid words and a television. He's in with the wrong lot, Emlyn. At that good school you are on about so often. He would never have taken that car but for Alun Poole and that John Brice. He'll end up in prison, that Brice boy, you mark my words. And so will our Geraint if we don't do something." She stared at her husband with watery-eyed frustration.

"I'll have a word with him, Gwen, I promise you. But not now. I've got a works meeting this morning, about this union trouble, see. I'll have a word with him at lunchtime."

Mr Rees made for the door, taking his heavy topcoat from the peg. He opened the door to the small front garden, rimmed by a low stone wall. The April sky was heavy and the wind was bringing sleet from the mountains, blowing in gusts between the grey stone cottages that lined the village's main street.

"Words, words, they never make bricks," said Mrs Rees, but her words were unheard as her husband stepped outside and closed the door behind him.

Gwen Rees turned and sat down in the chintz-covered armchair. It was Saturday and, by rights, she should have her man and her boy with her at home, helping her and talking together as a family should. Instead, her husband was attending a union meeting, in fear of redundancy, and her fifteen-year-old son was upstairs in disgrace, having been brought home the previous evening by the local police constable. For taking a car. Not so much stealing it, as taking it, getting into it and taking the handbrake off and steering it, freewheeling, for four miles down the valley until it stopped. No damage was done, the Lord be thanked, but the three boys responsible had had their names taken and been given a warning by the police. Next time, the juvenile court, PC Meredith had said. Gwen Rees blew her nose vigorously. A good thrashing was what the boy needed, from a stern father. She got to her feet wearily and began to busy herself with the chores. The Lord alone knew how it would end.

Upstairs, Geraint stared moodily out of the window. He had heard his father go out, and although the weather looked uninviting, even through the drifting sleet the distant mountains and the sheep paths winding at their feet called strongly. Chin cupped in hand, he gazed longingly and, hearing his mother clattering below, he came to a sudden decision.

Tossing away the comic he had read several times, he stood up and pulled on his sweater and his anorak. Quietly, he lifted the sash window.

"Stay in your room till you are told you can leave," his father had said.

"I'll show them I won't be treated like a child." Geraint ducked his head, cocked his leg over the sill and stepped on to the outhouse roof. The corrugated iron creaked as his weight went on to it, but he sat down and eased his way to the edge where he turned and, lowering himself carefully, dropped to the ground. In a crouching run, he vaulted the garden wall and went in among the bushes. Now he was free, the sleet was easing off, and there was nothing between him and the mountains. Strangely enough, he did not feel free.

He walked, kicking stones as he went, his thoughts in a turmoil. It seemed as though the world was ganging up on him. For months now he had felt hemmed in and picked on, at home and at school. The teachers had it in for him; his parents constantly nagged him and now this latest bit of trouble, a harmless prank that caused no damage to anyone or anything, and everyone behaved as though the world had come to an end. His eyes filled with tears. He would clear off, that's what he would do, if they didn't let up on him. Clear off to Manchester or Liverpool or London even.

He left the road and took the path along the bank of the Afon Carfan. The narrow river, normally little more than a stream, was now swollen by the rains so that in places it overflowed on to the path. Skirting these flooded areas, he crossed by the small stone bridge and was heading up the slope when a sound stopped him in his tracks. It was a bird cry, harsh and unmistakable. He looked up. There, high above him, was the shape of a raven; a jagged-winged, wedge-tailed black silhouette circling slowly, seemingly impervious to the strong gusts of wind. He watched it descending and as it

10

came closer to the scree at the foot of Craig-y-Cigfran, his interest mounted. He had long known there was a nest on the ledge high up and inaccessible among the crags, for he had watched the comings and goings of a pair of ravens many times. But it was unusual to see one come down so close to the road, especially when a human was so near. Then, even as he watched, the bird landed. It stood for a moment, turning its head this way and that, before hopping away to disappear among the rocks. Having nothing better to do, Geraint headed in the same direction.

He was about fifty metres from the spot where the bird had landed when it rose with a squawk of alarm from the scree to his right. To his surprise, it did not make off up the mountain but headed purposefully towards him. Geraint halted, non-plussed. The big bird was coming for him at head height. He gave a yell and ducked, throwing his arms above his head for protection. He felt as well as heard the whistling whirr of the wings as they brushed past him.

Geraint turned, his heart thumping. The bird was circling to renew the attack. Though frightened, Geraint felt anger at his own panic. He yelled again, but this time rushed forward, waving his arms. The great bird swerved and, whether deliberately or accidently the boy never knew, a trailing claw tore the back of his hand.

Geraint yelled again, this time with pain as well as anger. He glanced at the scratch, stooped and picked up a stone. The raven was turning, but this time much higher and further off. It came towards him but this was clearly more a gesture than an attack, for it lifted high above his head, avoiding the stone that Geraint hurled, with a casual, contemptuous tilt of its wing.

"You black devil," Geraint shouted. "Clear off!"

He felt better for shouting. His fear was replaced by aggression. The bird soared, croaking agitatedly, making

11

mock stoops that passed far above his head. Geraint took a deep breath, savouring his victory. The scratch on his hand was like a deep bramble scratch, nothing more. A battle scar, that's what it was. He wrapped his handkerchief around his hand and pressed on up the slope.

It took him five minutes to spot the young raven, cowering silent with beak agape between two rocks. The bird above called harshly but Geraint took no notice. He approached the motionless fledgeling with caution, for with the brown feathers fluffed out it looked as big as the parent bird and Geraint was wary of the huge bill. But he could see the blood on it, on its beak and on its breast. Crouching, he reached out slowly and the bird remained passive. When Geraint lifted it carefully with both hands, he noticed the unnatural angle of the right leg. The bird opened and closed its beak but made no sound.

"You've got a broken leg there, boyo," said Geraint, softly. "You won't last long out here with that."

He placed the bird on the ground and, taking off his anorak, laid it out. He moved the bird on to it and wrapped the quilted garment around it. Carrying it like a padded bag, he set out for home.

When he reached the one and only main street of Carfan, he quickened his step as he passed his house. There was no qualified vet in the village but Ma Lewis would know what to do. Most of the villagers bypassed the vet anyway with their injured pets and animals and took them instead to Ma Lewis. The old healing power, they said she had.

At the Carfan Arms, he turned off the main street and followed the narrow road for nearly a mile. Then, taking the lane signposted to the ancient standing stones, he arrived at the row of single-storey stone cottages. Ma Lewis had the end one, with a bit of ground where she kept the wildlife invalids that were brought to her. He could see a ewe with a bandaged leg tethered to a peg and heard a dog barking as he approached.

She came to the door before he knocked: a short, stocky, round-faced woman wearing an old-style thick black dress that reached to the ground, and over it a coarse-knitted black cardigan. She glanced at the bundled anorak in his hand and motioned him inside.

"On the table there, Geraint."

He put the bundle gently down. She didn't ask what was in it. She unwrapped it and stared at the young raven without a change of expression. While she stood there, Geraint glanced around. Like many of the old cottages in the village, there was just one large room with a small bedroom leading off. The big room served as kitchen and living room and at first glance, this one looked untidy and ill-kept. But this was because there was so much in it. In addition to the huge iron cooking-range and the table and chair and wooden rocking-chair and the

sink in the corner, there were cabinets and shelves on the walls
stacked with boxes and containers and jars. Below them were
several large wooden chests; bunches of various herbs hung
from the beams; two birdcages were hanging in the window
recess, in one a linnet, in the other a goldfinch. In another
time, Geraint reflected, say two centuries ago, it would have
seemed like the parlour of a witch. He tried to dismiss the
thought as he watched her attending the patient.

Without touching, she bent and examined the bird,
walking all round the table, her face at times getting
dangerously close to the heavy bill. The bird made no
movement save the blinking of its dove-grey eyes. Then the
woman went to a drawer and took out, of all things, an eye-
dropper. She filled the dropper from a cup of water at the
sink, then she put on some gloves she took from the shelf and
returned to the table. With a quick movement, she grasped
the bird's beak. Prising the dropper in at the hinge of the
beak, she let the bird drink. She refilled the dropper and
repeated the procedure until the bird's thirst seemed satisfied.

"Shock makes them drink," she said. "He has cracked his
leg, see, and something has bitten him, *bronwen* or *ffwlbart*, I
shouldn't wonder. You did well to keep him warm. They
often die soon after, but they are tough birds, these. They are
Welsh, you see."

Geraint chuckled, his relief bubbling out of him. More
than anything, he wanted that bird to live. He watched in
silence now as the deft hands of the old woman went to work.

"It's lucky it's the lower leg, just the single bone, see. I'll put
a splint on to keep it straight, help him to hop on it. He'll not
be flying properly yet, not a fledgeling like this, but he'll not
be long, judging from his feathers."

As she talked, she fetched a piece of split bamboo from the
shelf and a pack of lint. To Geraint's surprise, she handed
him an old woollen sock.

"Over his head, boy, while I tape him. That way he'll keep still."

Geraint, wary of the beak, dropped the sock over the bird's head and held it firmly. The blindfolded bird ceased moving at once. With quick hands the old woman wrapped a layer of lint round the leg, carefully positioned the short splint between the ankle-joint and the joint above and bound it firmly with sticky tape. While she worked, she kept up a sort of humming chant, a soothing, lilting flow of garbled Welsh that Geraint could not understand. The bird sat motionless until Geraint removed the sock. The raven lunged vainly with half-open beak as the woman stepped back.

"There, my treasure, now you'll be King of the Crows and live to be a hundred, eh?"

She laughed and Geraint chuckled again. It seemed to him the bird already looked more bright-eyed.

Now Geraint asked the questions that he had been wanting to ask while the woman had worked; about the care of the bird; where to keep it; how to feed it. He listened attentively to her answers and agreed to bring back the bird in four weeks' time to have the splint removed. When they had finished talking, he wrapped the bird up again in his anorak.

At the top of the lane, he turned to wave but the woman was nowhere to be seen. He made his way slowly homewards, going over in his mind what he was going to say to his parents.

Wrapped in the anorak, Corax endured the swaying motion without too much discomfort. His leg pained him less now that the bone was firmly splinted. Eventually, the motion stopped. He was set down again and the wrap was parted so that air could reach him. Some time elapsed before he was moved again and this time, when he was put down, the wrap was removed completely. He found himself on the ground;

hard, grass-tufted earth completely enclosed by wire mesh. He stayed where he was, turning his head, eyeing his surroundings.

He was in a rectangular pen, at one end of which was a wooden box on its side, the floor covered by an old blanket, tattered and crumpled. Two white faces above him watched as he stretched his wings cautiously, and tentatively tested his weight on the splinted limb. He shook himself and then began to hop awkwardly round the enclosure, exploring every corner. A bowl of water stood invitingly by the box and he sipped daintily, raising his head to let the water run down his throat. Then he picked the bowl up in his beak and turned it upside down, emptying the contents.

Now he explored the inside of the box. He lifted the blanket, examining it, and found he could tear it easily, which he proceeded to do with careful precision, bundling the tattered strips into a nest-like heap.

There was a movement above and a lamb-bone landed on the ground. He hopped to it and, picking off the meaty fragments, swallowed them hungrily. The two faces above stayed a while longer, then disappeared. Corax was alone in his new home. From far away, high in the misty cloud, came the call of an adult raven, and Corax chittered softly to himself.

3. Village Life

As the days passed, Corax grew accustomed to a routine of feeding and of receiving human visitors. The boy was the most frequent and Corax was soon taking food from his hand. The others when they came stared down at him and made clucking noises but no attempt at contact. From the start, Corax adapted to his new surroundings without hardship. Although he was confined, there was room enough in the pen to stretch his wings. He still avoided putting weight on his splinted leg but he was able to hop round the enclosure, which he frequently did, scratching at the grass for insects with his beak.

He quickly learned to recognise the features of his new way of life; to distinguish the footfalls of the boy from those of other humans; the sound of the kitchen door opening and shutting, which meant a visitor was coming his way; the rattle of the bucket bringing fresh water or the chink of crockery which signified a plate of scraps. Food was his main interest and he grew sleek and overweight.

There was another visitor, too. Kra. The old bird circled each day high above the village, unnoticed by the human

17

inhabitants, and when all was still, usually soon after dawn or at dusk, he would descend and call to the captive young raven. Corax would answer with agitated squawks and Kra would perch on the low wall beside the pen, or on the toolshed at the side of the small garden. If a human appeared, attracted by the young bird's cries, Kra would hop silently down the other side of the wall, flying off again when all was calm. Soon Corax gave up crying loudly for food every time he saw the parent bird and instead, answered with quiet utterances; in this way, the visits of Kra attracted no attention.

After a week in the pen, Corax was given greater, though not complete, freedom. He came to the boy's hand to snatch the morsel of mutton fat as he had so many times before, only to find himself gently but firmly grasped and lifted out of the pen. A piece of string was tied to his good leg and he was set down on the open ground. The small garden consisted of a patchy lawn with a narrow flowerbed around the edge below the low stone wall, and a rockery bordering the path to the shed. Corax found he could hop almost to the wall before the string, attached to a peg driven firmly into the ground, pulled him up. The restraint irritated him. Lowering his head, he severed the cord with one snip of his bill. The gasp of horror from the boy meant nothing to him. Now he could hop further and proceeded to shear the heads off the daffodils. He spotted a beetle which he followed with keen interest, not attacking it, across the grass. The boy approached, calling and coaxing, and sat down on the rockery. Corax jumped on to his shoulder where he stayed, liking the warmth of the face against his body and *pruking* softly as the boy's hand gently smoothed him under his beak. Hands then carefully lifted him back into the pen and his first taste of freedom was over.

A few days later, during the first week of May, Corax was let out again. His first movement was to the crouching boy's

pocket where he knew the chocolate drops would be. His head delved and sure enough, his prying beak extracted the ever-present titbit which he crunched appreciatively. Then he fluttered towards the wall. A strong hop and he was up on it, where the wind from the mountains ruffled his feathers and he could see through the bushes to the valley beyond.

Behind him, with bated breath, stood the boy, watching. Corax hopped down the other side of the wall. He was in open country now, his wings fledged sufficiently for a trial flight. But the young raven had no such desire. The boy was imprinted as the provider of his food and there was no need to fly. Besides, there were new discoveries to make, starting with the blossom on the blackthorn bushes. Stretching to the lowermost branches, he began snipping off the flowers one by one, causing a shower of white petals.

The game soon palled. A blackbird scuttled, shrilling with alarm, from below one bush to another and Corax hopped in playful pursuit. The blackbird, not appreciating the sport, flew with strident agitation for safety in the higher branches.

For over an hour Corax explored the stony wasteland,

before the rattle of spoon on plate drew him back over the wall to the garden. There, he was given more chocolate drops than he had ever been given at one time, before being returned to his pen. Contented, he sat inside the box to rest after his exertions.

The following week, the wire round the box was removed and Corax was free to come and go as he liked. His leg had been in the splint less than three weeks and already he could put almost as much weight on it as on his sound leg.

Although he was now fully fledged and had total freedom, he made no attempt to leave, even when Kra paid his visits before the village awoke. Once, the old bird descended at dusk, calling insistently, but Corax simply crouched by his bowl, sated from a feed, and croaked drowsily. The adult bird flew silently away.

The freedom, however, did give Corax a new lease of life. He was able to follow the boy more often and more closely. Reluctant to lose sight of him, he would bound in pursuit when the boy returned to the house after leaving him a bowl of food. At first, he was not allowed into the house, but after a few days he managed to flutter up to the kitchen windowsill and enter through the open window. The boy caught him drinking milk from a jug and put him outside. After that, he was allowed into the kitchen but only when someone was there to watch him.

When he was shut outside, Corax found, by listening carefully, that he could hear the boy leave the house by the front door. This led him to discover that by hopping round the side of the house he could follow the boy up the main street to where he and the other children were picked up by the school bus. Corax became a familiar sight, bounding awkwardly behind the boy, wings akimbo, finally fluttering up and perching on the boy's shoulder until the bus came. Corax would then return to the garden to spend the day until he made his way to the front wall again to meet the boy off the bus at the regular time in the late afternoon. With excited *pruk, pruking* he would delve into the pocket for chocolate drops.

With each day that passed, the young raven grew bolder and more adventurous. One morning, when the boy disappeared into the bus as usual, Corax fluttered from the wall to the top of the old-fashioned, single-decker bus where he perched happily on the luggage rack until the boy disembarked outside the school in the neighbouring village. Corax hopped down and landed on the startled boy's shoulder. He was not given any chocolate drops. Instead, he was held firmly by the boy and was put on to a similar bus that was heading back towards the boy's home. So Corax rode back and when the bus stopped in the main street, he fluttered to the familiar wall of his own accord, saving the driver the trouble of putting him there.

The next day, the same thing happened, only this time, when the bus stopped at the school and the boy and his friends stepped off, the other bus was there and Corax simply fluttered across to the top of it, ready for the ride back. The ride became a daily ritual and Corax learned to recognise the other bus so that, if they passed on the road, he would flutter across to the approaching bus as it went by and remain perched on top for the journey back. Though he did not know it, Corax was soon the talk of both villages.

The school bus pulled in as usual and Geraint stepped off, waiting until it had moved away before crossing the road. He looked along the wall where his pet was usually waiting and his heart missed a beat when he could not see him. He quickened his step and as he neared his house, at the end of a long line of identical stone-built houses, he saw a movement in the bushes near the back garden wall. A man was there and he appeared to be feeding his bird, for the raven was on the wall stretching and bobbing to the man's outstretched hand. Geraint gave a whistle, the one he always used, and the bird instantly fluttered along the wall towards him. The man turned and saw Geraint and hurried off into the bushes. Geraint shrugged. He had recognised him. It was Old Tom Davis, a local eccentric – some said simpleton – who lived on his own in an isolated cottage on the outskirts of the village. He was harmless enough. Geraint forgot his as the bird hopped closer, fluttered the remaining distance and landed heavily on his shoulder.

"Hello, Corbie boy, hello then."

The bird produced a constant flow of soft clacking sounds as he pressed his side against the boy's warm face. The two moved round the side of the house to the garden and Corax hopped down the outstretched arm and pushed his head into the jacket pocket. He emerged with a chocolate drop which he crunched greedily.

They played for a while, the boy sitting on the wall and throwing a plastic clothes-peg which the bird retrieved, bringing it back to the boy's feet. Geraint never ceased to be amazed at the bird's intelligence.

Unknown to him as he played, Geraint's parents were watching from the kitchen where his mother was preparing the tea.

"Finding that bird has been the making of him, Emlyn. He's a different boy."

"You're right, Gwen. The responsibilities of ownership, it is. Takes his mind off other things, gives him an outlet, see."

Emlyn Rees sounded pleased. He did not like scenes and he had not had to give his son a talking to after all. His wife could tell he was relieved but she didn't mind. What mattered was that Geraint had shown a remarkable change of attitude. His unusual pet had made him the focus of attention with his schoolmates and there was no doubt that having a creature dependent upon him had focused his own attention, giving him a purpose where before there had been aimlessness. She still wished she could have had more children, for being one of six herself, she had never known the isolation of an only child within a family. But she had learned to live with the regret. Certainly the bird could not have arrived at a more opportune time and as she watched them playing together, she marvelled at the bond they seemed to have between them.

Not that she had taken to the bird at first. When she had first discovered the boy's disobedience and his escape, a wave of depression, even fear, had come over her. Her fear had been that he had run away. When he had returned, even before her husband had come back from his meeting, she had tried hard not to show her relief. She had remonstrated with him, but his concern for the bird that he had taken to Ma Lewis was so evident that she had decided to make little of his rebelliousness, and persuaded her husband to do the same. From that day, the boy's surliness had begun to fade and it was evident that, by sharing his interest, the three were becoming united again.

But she could not take to the bird itself. She was nervous of it. Ravens had a reputation for evil, for cunning and for being prophets of doom. Try as she would to like it, even feeding it from her hand, it had only to turn that implacable grey eye to meet her gaze and she at once had the shivers. Long-forgotten memories of the big black bird winging its way through the mists of the ancient Celtic legends she had heard as a girl swirled back into her mind and filled her with suspicion. But this was something she would not admit to anyone.

Geraint was coming up to the house now and she turned from the window to see to the meal.

The three sat round the table. The raven had been ushered from the kitchen door and was perched on the toolshed from where it could see in through the window. The roosting box with its blanket bedding had been put on the shed roof to which he could flutter from the wall.

"I caught old Daffy Davis with Corbie just now," said Geraint, sipping his tea. "I think he must have been feeding him."

"That's funny," said his father. "I saw him skulking in the bushes down the side there yesterday. I wondered what he was doing. It didn't occur to me he was with the bird."

"Well now, there's a strange thing." Geraint's mother looked at both of them. "I came back from the shops on Monday and he was sitting on our wall. Gave me a wave, he did, and I waved back and why shouldn't I? Everyone knows he's harmless enough." She turned to Geraint. "And you shouldn't call him Daffy, Geraint. It isn't nice and it isn't true. Old Tom is what he is called. He may be a bit strange but he isn't stupid. He's had a tragic life, from all I hear."

"Oh, everyone at school calls him Daffy, Mam. He talks to himself and Martin told me he lets his goat live in the house with him."

Geraint began to chuckle but checked it at the look from his mother.

"No need to be unkind about him, Geraint," his father put in, mildly. "Your mother's right. There's no harm in him. Old Tom is a nicer name, I think. And if he wants to see your bird, I don't see any harm in it."

Geraint shrugged. "I don't mind him looking, Da. But I don't want him feeding him. He might give him something poisonous by mistake. If you see him, tell him he can look but not to feed him."

His mother nodded. "That's fair enough. I'll tell him if he comes again. Poor man, I feel sorry for him. He was born

24

near here, I heard, in one of the villages. Went away, during the war, he did, no one knows where. Some say he was a prisoner, some say . . . well, some say anything, don't they? Kindness costs nothing now, does it?"

Geraint, holding out his plate, nodded in agreement. "Can I have some more cake, Mam?"

4. Strange Encounters

Geraint thought no more about Old Tom until he returned home the following evening. Sitting having his tea as usual (his father had been delayed at work by yet another meeting), he listened to his mother describe the chief events of her day. Or rather, event; for one incident dominated all others.

"I don't know what it is with Old Tom and your bird, Geraint, but I caught him round here again today. Lunchtime, it was, and I had nipped across to see Mrs Baker. When I came back, I found the poor man in the kitchen here, and your bird up on the dresser. I said to him, 'Now then Old Tom, just what are you doing here?' And he said, 'Sorry to intrude, Mrs Rees, but the bird came in and I thought I'd better get him out for you.' So I said, 'I expect he'll go out when you go out, Old Tom,' and sure enough, when he left, the bird hopped down and went after him, out to his box on the shed.''

She paused for breath and a sip of tea. "So I called after him, I said, 'Tom Davis, don't you be letting the bird into the house now.' And when he had gone, I thought to myself, now did I leave our back door open or didn't I? I usually close it but I can't swear to it. It was a warm day and I have it open when the sun is there, see. He has certainly taken to your bird, Geraint, Old Tom has. Can't seem to see enough of it. But he's harmless, I'm sure. I feel so sorry for him."

Geraint shrugged. He felt a resentment towards the man that was hard to explain. Corbie was his pet, no one else's, and the man seemed to be treating him as though he was his.

"Silly old fool should keep away, Mam. Walking into people's houses like that, he has no right. He should stop hanging around the house and the bird. I shall tell him when I see him."

"Now don't be unkind, Geraint. The poor man, he cannot help himself entirely. He does no harm, I'm sure of it."

Geraint grunted and finished his cup of tea.

"I'm going to do my prep now. After, I'm going round to Martin's to play some records."

"Then don't you be late, Geraint. And don't rush your work. You know how important that is."

Geraint winced as he went upstairs to his room. He really didn't need to be told that his work was important, but tell him they did, all the time, without ceasing, at school by day and at home by night. He felt his old rebelliousness returning.

Geraint worked at his homework without enthusiasm. He had mislaid his watch that morning and could only guess the time, but after about an hour he closed his books and went downstairs. He tried to leave quietly by the front door but his father called out.

"That you, Geraint? Done your prep, have you?"

"Yes, Da." He opened the door.

"Well, I hope you've done it properly. Don't be late now."

Geraint stepped outside and almost slammed the door but thought better of it. He closed it very quietly.

He found Martin, who lived at the other end of the village, by himself in the house, his parents having gone out. Martin

27

was his closest schoolfriend and the possessor of a large collection of records of all kinds. Martin's father was renowned for his home-brewed beer and the outhouse at the back was stacked with filled vats of it. Geraint was offered a glass as soon as he arrived and, having been reassured that Martin's father wouldn't mind, he willingly had his glass refilled at increasingly frequent intervals while they listened to the records. Geraint's mood did not lend itself to caution. The alcoholic content of the unusually potent brew did not take effect for an hour or so, but by the time darkness was setting in, it dawned on him that he was not his usual self. He rose to leave and had difficulty with his balance. Outside, the fresh air helped and he hurried as directly as his strangely independent feet would let him along the road towards his house.

By now the eastern sky was dark and the pink from the west behind the crest of Foel Ddu was fading rapidly. He stopped, leaning on a wall, and took a deep breath, blinking hard to keep the view of the cottages on the slope above the river in focus. The earth was billowing gently, like an ocean in a quiet breeze, and a night-black fog was rolling along the valley from the crags, cloaking the regimented line of cottage chimneypots.

Gradually, the mist lifted and parted like a curtain and Geraint found himself gazing at an ordered line of glinting helmets, some with plumes, some without. They were undulating with the horses' movements as the riders advanced along the valley. Now he could see the glinting cuirasses and the flashing harness bangles of the bedecked mounts. Here and there a waving standard fluttered from a legionnaire's lance and at intervals through the mist, chariot wheels spun like silver discs. Geraint straightened up from the wall, his eye taking in the countless marchers who stretched the valley's length and at a moment when the swirling mist cleared totally for a moment, he could even see the raven circling high above the moving column. Then the fog closed and obliterated everything, matching the darkness of his own closed eyes. When he opened them, only the smoky wisps from the scarcely visible chimneypots moved between him and the mountains, though by now he was barely able to grasp what was reality or fantasy. He moved on slowly, steadying himself against the wall as he went, until he reached his own front gate. The hall light was on behind the front door so his parents were still up. Shaking his head to clear it, he decided to go round the back. Perhaps he could creep in without disturbing them.

He opened the gate to go down the side path. A movement caught his eye. On the shed roof was the shape of a big black bird, watching him. Geraint put his fingers to his lips.

"Hello, Corbie. No noise now, Corbie."

The bird hopped to the edge of the roof.

"Hello, Blackie," said the raven. "Hello, boyo. Blackie boy."

The voice was deep, rasping and metallic and not of this world. Geraint stopped, petrified, his heart palpitating, his head swimming.

"Hello, Blackie. Blackie, Blackie, Blackie."

The bird's voice ceased abruptly and opening both wings, so that they spanned the width of the shed, the great shape lifted off, blackening the sky, obliterating the last vestiges of clear thought that were trying to tell him that this could not be happening. As the bird rose and became one with the night, the world span so fast that Geraint fell to the ground.

How long he stayed there, on his hands and knees, Geraint never knew. But his breath returned and his heartbeat quietened and he picked himself up. Unable to comprehend anything any more, he found his way to the back door and let himself into the kitchen.

29

The light was on and his mother was there, laying the table in readiness for breakfast.

"This is too late for you, Geraint," she said. "You've got school tomorrow and . . . ."

She broke off when she turned and looked at him. "Geraint, what's the matter?"

He sat down on a chair, white and shaking. When his mother put her arm round to steady him, she smelt the beer on his breath.

"Oh, I see, it's the drink now is it? You have been on the beer, have you? Well, you will get no sympathy from me. Serves you right, boy, that's what I say. I hope you are sick, then perhaps you will not be so foolish."

Geraint, who felt his senses returning, made no attempt to reply. Instead, he bent to unlace his shoes. His mother, seeing his colour beginning to return, kept her heart hard and left him. There was no point in reprimanding him now, not in the state he was in. The morning would do. She went up the stairs, shaking her head. Just when he had seemed more settled, he was coming home drunk. Who would have children?

From the kitchen, Geraint, still unable to think clearly, made his way up to bed. Sleep was all he wanted; sleep to still the pounding in his head and calm the turmoil of his mind.

Next morning, with a heavy head, Geraint prepared for school as usual. At breakfast, he listened resignedly to the telling off his parents gave him. He said nothing, needing a longer, quieter time to think about the extraordinary incident of the previous night. At the moment, he was unable to decide whether he had imagined everything. He rose from the table, looking round the kitchen.

"Seen my watch, Mam? I left it here yesterday morning,

after I took it off to wash my hands."

"Yes, I put it on the shelf. I remember because I had to put the . . ."

She broke off, staring at the shelf. "Has anyone taken the two fifty-pence pieces I left here on top of the milk bill? I owe the milkman, I put them there yesterday." She looked on the other shelves and on the dresser.

"And your watch has gone, too." She turned to her husband. "Emlyn, you haven't moved some money and a watch, have you?"

"No, of course I haven't. You have another look, Gwen, they'll be behind something else."

His wife began moving objects when a sudden exclamation from Geraint stopped her in her tracks.

"It's Old Tom!" Geraint faced his parents, an angry look on his face. "He was in here yesterday. He's taken the money and the watch."

There was a silence as his parents took this in. Without speaking, they both began a thorough search. Ten minutes later, Geraint's father turned to his wife.

"They're not here, Gwen. I think Geraint is right. It's too much of a coincidence."

His wife looked near to tears. "And I've always felt so sorry for him. The wretched man, he's not too simple to be a thief. I'll feel sorry for him when I see him again, I can tell you."

"Look, Mam, I can't stop now, I'll miss the bus. We'll have another look this evening."

Geraint packed his homework in his duffle-bag and went out to feed the raven. The bird was on the shed roof and hopped to his shoulder as he approached. Geraint put down a bowl of scraps but the bird stayed with him as he hurried to the street and along to the bus. As usual, the raven travelled on top of the bus and returned on the incoming one. Once back in the garden, he chased away the starlings round the

31

food bowl and settled down to clear every last crumb.

Geraint arrived back at half past four. As he crossed the road, he saw Tom Davis on the other side of the garden wall with the raven feeding from his hand.

Geraint thought quickly. He headed up the road so that he could cross the wasteland and approach the man from behind. He moved quietly but the man heard him and turned long before he reached him.

"Hang on, Old Tom, I want to talk to you."

Geraint's call prevented the man from making off. He stood, waiting, as Geraint came up to him. Geraint took in the man's shabby jacket and shirt and worn trousers and the stubble on his chin. Yet he was clean and from his lined face, his brown eyes faced him steadily. Geraint had to steel himself to say what he had to say.

"Look, Old Tom, have you found a watch and some

money? It's missing from our kitchen and you were in there yesterday."

A shadow passed over the man's face and his eyes creased slightly.

"No, I have not, young Rees. I have not found a watch or any money and if I had I would not have taken them. I am not a thief, see."

"Well, you were in our kitchen and so was the watch and the money and now they've gone."

The man stared at him, saying nothing, and Geraint saw his mouth was quivering. Then he turned and walked away without speaking.

"You keep out of our house, do you hear?" Geraint called after him. "And keep away from my bird, too. We don't want you round here, see, none of us, so just you keep away."

The departing figure hesitated but did not turn, and disappeared into the bushes. The raven fluttered up to Geraint's shoulder as he stepped over the wall and into the garden. There, he played with the bird for a while, hiding chocolate drops for him to find, before going indoors.

He told his mother what had occurred while they sat outside in the sun on two kitchen chairs, drinking their tea. As they sat, they watched the raven lifting up stones on the rockery and snatching up beetles. The bird tired of this and hopped up to Geraint's chair. He perched on his knee and deftly snatched the spoon from Geraint's saucer.

"Now then, Corbie, just you give that back!"

Geraint reached out but the bird, sensing a game, hopped down and fluttered up to the shed roof. Laughing, Geraint got up and followed him. He grabbed at the raven but the bird dodged expertly and, with the spoon in his beak, retreated to his roosting box where he thrust the spoon under the tattered blanket on the floor.

"Oh, Corbie, you are a nuisance." Geraint, grumbling

33

half-heartedly, carried the kitchen chair across to the shed so that he could stand on it and reach into the box. All the time the raven was chuckling as though enjoying the joke.

Geraint reached under the blanket and froze. He stayed motionless for so long that his mother called out.

"Is something wrong, Geraint?"

Geraint pulled the box towards him and lifted up the blanket. His mother, puzzled, crossed over to him. He handed something down and she took it, wonderingly. Into her outstretched hand he put a watch, then the spoon, then half a dozen bottle tops. Silent, she put them down on the grass. Geraint handed her some clothes-pegs, a nail file, a piece of broken glass, two fifty-pence pieces, a broken shoe buckle and a ballpoint pen. Satisfied he had missed nothing, Geraint stepped down from the chair. The bird hopped up and down excitedly, uttering a constant bubbling call.

Geraint and his mother stared at each other.

"Now what do I do, Mam? I called Old Tom a thief to his face. I should have thought of Corbie. He was in the kitchen, you said so. What do I do, Mam?"

Geraint, picking up the raven's hoard, followed his mother into the house.

"You apologise, Geraint," she said. "The poor man, he was doing no harm at all. You must go round to him straight away and apologise for me and your father as well, for we all thought it. Oh, what a dreadful thing to do to the poor man."

There was a raucous chittering from behind and Geraint turned to see the culprit flutter down from the roof to resume the beetle hunt among the rockery stones.

"And what do I do about you, Corbie? Your splint comes off soon. You're the only pet I've had. I don't know why you haven't flown off already. If I don't clip your wings, you'll be gone. What do I do about that, Mam?"

His mother shook her head. "That is something you must decide, Geraint. He's your pet. Your father and I will be happy for him to stay if you do clip his wings but we've agreed that the decision must be yours."

Geraint watched the raven's antics and shrugged before turning and going indoors.

5. *Old Tom's Story*

Geraint worked at his homework that evening with only half his mind on it. The recollection of the man's hurt eyes, blinking at him like a wounded animal's, floated across the paper in front of him. At six o'clock he closed his books and hurried downstairs. His father, when he had learned of the discoveries, had echoed his mother's view, that an apology should be delivered to Tom Davis as soon as possible.

Taking his light anorak, for the evening was cool, Geraint headed down the village street. He knew where Old Tom lived, a little more than a mile off the main road, just past the lane that led to the ancient standing stones and Ma Lewis's cottage. His cottage stood in an isolated hollow close to the raised earthworks of an ancient fort, now overgrown with bracken.

As he walked, turning off past the Carfan Arms, Geraint went over his apology in his mind. His thoughts were interrupted by the sudden screams of peewits rising from the field. Glancing over the low wall, he saw a black cat stalking through the grass among the sheep. The sheep took no notice but the birds circled, calling loudly until the cat had jumped the far wall and disappeared. Geraint watched the handsome green-and-white birds settle again and run through the grass, their crested heads bobbing and vanishing.

He stopped at the bend in the road as a crow flew overhead, cawing harshly. The sight of it, a smaller version of the raven, reminded him of Corbie and of the question he knew he must face: whether to clip the bird's wings and so condemn him to a life of domesticity, or to let him enjoy, as that crow was enjoying, the freedom of the air.

He walked on, pondering. Soon he could see the cottage, a hundred metres from the road, below the terraced mound of the ancient earthworks. Turning into the gateway, he went down the long path. Near the house, a stone wall surrounded an orchard in which a score of bantams scattered, clucking, at his approach.

As he approached the house, the figure of Tom Davis appeared in the doorway.

"'Day, young Rees. Come to see me, have you? Unexpected this is."

Geraint faced him. "I've come to see you, Old Tom, to apologise. I made a false accusation against you and very ashamed I am. I had no right to accuse you like I did. We have found the missing articles, see, and I should not have called you a thief. My mother and father both thought like I did and I am to give you their apologies as well. I hope you will accept them and . . . well, it is very, very sorry we are."

Geraint's prepared piece came to an end. He waited, tongue-tied and embarrassed. The man's level stare unnerved him. He turned to leave.

"I accept your apology, young Rees, and you can tell your mam and da that I accept theirs. You had no right to say such things without proof, see. Have you found what was missing?"

"Yes, and other things besides. And you'll never guess where they were, Old Tom . . ."

Geraint broke off. The man was nodding and smiling.

"Indeed I can. The bird. They are alike, the birds." He was talking more to himself than Geraint. He looked up. "It was the bird, wasn't it?"

"Yes, it was. But how did you know?"

The man stared at him. "You had best come inside, young Rees. No need to talk out here."

Geraint followed him. The orchard was unkempt, the grass long, the path weed-covered. The smallholding was too much for one man to cope with. But the bantams scuttling round his feet were plump and glossy-feathered and among the apple trees he saw a row of beehives. The air was scented with apple blossom. The bleat of a goat came from behind the cottage. Though the land was untended, the man evidently cared for his livestock.

Inside the living room, Geraint was struck by the contrast to the interior of Ma Lewis's cottage, so cluttered and crowded. This was spartan in comparison, and clean and tidy; a wooden table, one chair and a bench, nothing on the walls, a Welsh dresser and a threadbare carpet on the stone floor. A grandfather clock stood next to the fireplace, incongruous in the sparsely furnished low-ceilinged room, and its loud ticking echoed in the confined space.

"Sit down, young Rees. Tell me, how did you come by the bird?"

Geraint sat on the bench while the man took the chair.

"I found him, Old Tom, found him with his leg broken up on the slope under Craig-y-Cigfran and Ma Lewis set him in a splint. It's coming off tomorrow. He hasn't flown yet, for some reason, but he could any time. I must get his wings clipped or he'll be off and I'll not see him again."

The man sat staring at him, nodding. Although his attitude, his mannerisms, were odd, unlike those of other folk, Geraint felt no nervousness. Truth to tell, there was something reassuring about the man, with his steady gaze. His reactions were hard to predict and Geraint felt slightly uncomfortable at the prolonged silence. Uncomfortable, but not apprehensive. For whatever folk said, this quiet, calm old man with his shabby clothes and clean, tidy cottage was no simpleton and Geraint felt shame that he had called him Daffy.

The man seemed to reach a decision.

"I will tell a story, young Rees. About the bird, see. Your bird. Any bird. About clipping their wings."

Geraint nodded, intrigued and willing to listen.

Again a long silence, broken only by the ticking of the clock.

"It is like my bird, see. Your black bird is like mine. All that time ago. How old are you, boy?"

"I'm fifteen."

"Fifteen, is it? Well, I was eighteen, see. And I lived in Gorwyr."

Geraint started. Gorwyr was a village only four miles away.

"Yes, not many round here know that, young Rees, for all their knowledge of other people. And a different man I was then, not the ageing, tired man you see now, I can tell you." He gave a wry smile. "And the young tearaway I was then took a dare, see, a dare no one else would take. You know what it was?"

Geraint shook his head.

"Well, it was to climb Foel Ddu by the east face." He saw Geraint's incredulous look. "Yes indeed, you know where I mean. Where the quarry was. Six hundred feet sheer, granite polished like marble. To the raven's nest, see. For an egg. That was the dare, boy. At eighteen. There wasn't a man, let alone a boy, could climb Foel Ddu by that face. I did it. Like a fly, I was. Nerves of steel, I can tell you." He laughed. "Like an idiot, I was. No, not an idiot, just a boy. That's how I went up Foel Ddu. Like a boy."

He paused and Geraint waited.

"Well, I was up at the nest, see. And those birds came at me like demons from hell. Shrieking like fiends and pecking my hands, to make me drop, see, me clinging to the granite. You see that."

The man leaned towards Geraint, stretching out his arm. On his wrist, like a white, bleached leaf, was a long-healed scar. Geraint glanced down at his own hand, at the scratch he had received from the parent of his bird.

"But I got to the nest," the man continued. "They couldn't stop me, those black devils. Only there wasn't an egg. Just three young birds, nearly ready to fly. So what did I do? I took the biggest young bird and stuffed it into my jumper. Then I climbed down and won my dare."

The man, nodding, was lost in the reminiscence. Geraint waited, saying nothing.

"Kept him till he was fledged and ready to fly, I did. And I loved that bird. Loved him more than anything else in the world. If I had not had him . . ." He shrugged, leaving the consequence unspoken.

"I had the same decision, young Rees. Just the same as you have now. My best, my only companion. I could keep him by clipping his wings. Or I could leave him be and let him go. And I decided I could not do without him."

The man's voice descended to a whisper. "I even knew what part of the wing, what feathers I was going to clip. Quite painless, see. In the morning I would do it. But I never did. Because then came the day I . . . the day when . . . I went away." His dreamy look faded and he stared directly at Geraint.

"Yes, went away, I did, young Rees, went away for a long time. It was the war, see. Taken prisoner I was. Then I was ill. And if I had clipped his wings, he would have died or been killed, that is for sure. No one else to care for him. Did not like him, most of them. Feared him, even. But he could fly, see; free, like he was meant. Free to live his own life. And when I came back he was gone. More happy than sorry, I was, to find him gone. There's a power in a raven, young Rees, a power a man can't explain. But they can sense a man, see. They can tell the difference between us. Blackie now, he took to me, but not to others. We had a real understanding, him and me."

He was off again, into his reveries. Geraint frowned. Something nagged at him. Slowly, he straightened on his seat, his eyes widening in disbelief. He had almost missed it.

Collecting his thoughts, he chose his words carefully.

"Old Tom, what was his name? What did you call him, your bird?"

The man opposite focused on him. "Blackie, he was; as black as night, and he knew his name, see. He liked to say it, over and over. He could talk, you see, I taught him the words. We had an understanding."

The man leaned forward. "Are you taking the point, young Rees? Are you taking the reason for my story? Do not clip his wings. Do not take freedom from a bird, nor from a man. We can't see the future. Cruel and selfish it would be if you were to go, to leave the valley."

Geraint nodded, barely listening. His mind was elsewhere.

"Old Tom, can I tell you a story now? To do with ravens, or at least, one raven. One that can say 'Blackie, hello Blackie boy' over and over."

The man stared at him and his eyes narrowed. When he spoke, his voice was husky.

"What are you telling me, boy?"

Geraint took a deep breath. "Two nights ago, just as it was getting dark, I . . . I was not feeling well after a . . . after a party, and this bird, a big black raven, flew from the shed where I keep Corbie – that is what I call my bird – and it called out 'Hello, Blackie, hello Blackie boy, Blackie, Blackie, Blackie. Over and over, like you said."

Geraint paused. The man had put both hands flat down on

41

the table and sat staring at Geraint with an intentness that made him uncomfortable.

The gleam faded, though his body remained rigid. "I am sixty-two, young Rees. Older than I like to think but not as old as I look." He gave a rueful smile. "I took that bird from Foel Ddu forty-four years ago. Now you tell me he is still here. And I am saying there is a power in a raven. Forty-four years."

He stood up, shaking his head. "They do say ravens live as long as men. The truth is, they are older – older than men, than any man. Noah it was sent out a raven from the ark; and the ancient Romans told the future by them; and they came across the seas on the shoulders of the Vikings; the raven-god Odin himself kept them. They have fed the superstitions of men since Man began. Ah, young Rees, what has the eye of the raven not seen, eh?"

With the man standing over him, Geraint felt obliged to get to his feet. The talk of ancient times served as another reminder to Geraint and it was on the tip of his tongue to tell of the strange vision that had preceded his encounter with the bird, but he could not bring himself to speak of it. To tell of a bird he knew could be real was one thing; to tell of a vision after too much to drink, that was quite another.

Geraint followed the man outside and they stood on the path. The scent of apple blossom was strong and the air was heavy with the drone of bees winging to and from the hives. The bantams clucked sociably as they high-stepped round the man's feet, scratching in the dust. A magpie crossed between the trees.

"See that, young Rees. First cousin to the raven, he is. And master of his own fate because he is free, he can fly. Clip his wings and his freedom's gone. And what use is life without freedom, tell me that, eh?"

Geraint, whose mind was already made up, nodded.

"I'll not be cutting Corbie's wings, Old Tom. But what about your raven, your Blackie? What will I do if I see him again?"

The man scratched his chin reflectively. "Yes indeed, I would like to see Blackie again. Forty-four years – is it possible?" He eyed Geraint, askance. "You did not dream this, did you, boy?"

Geraint bit his lip. "No. No, I saw that bird, and heard it, I swear it. Perhaps he came to see Corbie."

"Perhaps, perhaps. Perhaps he came to persuade you not to clip your bird's wings, eh? There's a power in a raven, see. I will be watching out now for my Blackie, don't you worry. If he is about, I will know him all right, forty-four years or not."

"All right, Old Tom. I must go now." Geraint found himself reluctant to leave, but there was nothing to keep him.

"You tell your mam and da to watch their silver, see. While your bird is there, that is."

"I'll tell them." Geraint hurried off. At the gate he glanced back but the man had disappeared.

"While your bird is there." The words lingered with Geraint. Tomorrow the splint would come off, and the leg would be completely restored. Tomorrow might well be the last time he would see his bird.

6. *In the Wild*

The next day was Saturday. Geraint gave the bird its morning feed and lifting it from his shoulder where it had fluttered to perch, he placed in a cardboard carton. Then he set out for Ma Lewis's cottage.

She took the splint off in a few seconds. While Geraint held the bird, she felt along the leg bone and nodded, satisfied.

"As good as ever. A big, strong bird he is, too. It's a wonder he's not flown off before now. He obviously knows when he's well off."

Geraint thanked her profusely and gave her the homemade blackberry-and-apple wine that his mother had told him to give her. Her face lit up as she took it.

"Thank you, Geraint, and you thank your mam, now. And you had better clip your bird's wings if you want to keep him. He's relied on you longer than he need have done already. He'll be leaving any time now."

Geraint walked homewards with the bird on his shoulder. "If you want to keep him." Geraint felt a lump in his throat. Of course he wanted to keep him. His schoolfriends envied him, the whole village talked about him, but most of all, the bird provided him with companionship. He knew he was

44

going to feel lost without it. But his mind was made up. He looked across at the mountains, blue in the morning haze, stretching away to meet the sky. He would not deprive a bird of its natural right to soar above those mountains.

In the garden, he watched the bird discovering the new flexibility of the healed leg. Stretching it naturally, the raven put its full weight on it and bounded round the garden, fluttering from the wall to the shed and down again, chattering to itself and growing in confidence with every minute. Geraint resigned himself to his pet's almost instant departure.

But the bird did not leave. It flew to him at his call, landed on his outstretched arm and delved into his pocket for chocolate drops. Then it returned to the box on the shed. And in the afternoon, when Geraint returned from visiting, expecting to find it gone, he was surprised and pleased when the familiar shape came to his shoulder; not fluttering, but flying evenly from the shed with a strong wingbeat.

And the raven was there in the evening. Geraint fed it from his hand before letting it hop as usual to its roost in the box. And there he left it, squatting black and bright-eyed in the semi-darkness.

The bird stayed for ten more days, flying above the garden and the house, but always returning. On the morning of the eleventh day, Geraint went out as usual before breakfast to the shed. And because it was what he had been expecting, he felt no great shock when he discovered the bird had gone. Had he not dreamed last night that he heard its departing cry? Nothing, though, could alleviate his sense of loss. His raven had left him.

Corax awoke to the deep, harsh call of Kra, from the wall beside the shed. He emerged from the box, shaking his feathers, flexing the leg that had been held by the splint for so long. He flew down and settled beside the adult raven.

It was dawn, but the night had not yet left the valley. Kra gave another raucous croak, which caused the boy in the nearby house to stir restlessly in his sleep, and lifted off. Corax followed. The two ravens winged from the slumbering village towards the mountains.

Corax flew slowly, his flight ungainly. After only a few hundred metres, he tired. It was the furthest he had ever flown. He needed to rest. Gliding down, he settled on a rock near the rippling river.

Kra circled, *pruk pruking* with impatience. Corax sat with his wings outstretched like a cormorant until his strength returned. Then he rose and flew again after Kra.

Three times Corax stopped to rest. After each stop, he flew further than before. When he finally arrived at Craig-y-Cigfran, at the ledge where he had been born, he was exhausted.

He followed Kra down to the monument of twigs from which the other fledged young had long since flown. As he settled, another adult raven appeared from above and screamed disapproval. It was Vara, his mother, but there was nothing motherly about the way she drove him from his birthplace. Kra, whose persistent attention to his injured offspring had been prompted not only by instinct but also by a residual relationship with Man, or one man in particular, stayed on the ledge and preened himself. It was as though, now he had shown Corax the way to freedom and led him back to his birthplace from which, less than six weeks before, the fledgeling had been blown by the wind, his parental instinct had died. There he stayed as Vara drove the bewildered Corax from the ledge, out above the valley and the rock-strewn slopes. Corax, weary from the unaccustomed flights, descended to avoid the aerial buffeting of the adult raven and, as chance would have it, came to rest near the place where he had fallen as a fledgeling. There he cowered, trembling, until Vara, still giving voice to her aggression, rose and disappeared.

Corax was on his own now. Before him lay the world, bounded by horizons of jagged granite set against a brightening sky. The mountain breeze riffled his feathers as he called; and his call, his first assertive male *korronk*, carried like a challenge in the wind. He flapped his wings and lifted off, letting the air currents carry him above the valley and the stream, soaring, learning with instinctive immediacy to master the turbulence of the winds with subtle movements of his wings. His heavy body, supported by a wingspan well over a metre across, was buoyant and responsive and with every tilt of his wings his flight control and direction improved. Up he soared, then down, with only the smallest wingflick, his bubbling calls telling of his confidence. He veered towards the towering shape of Craig-y-Cigfran but from high above the peak, Vara, circling, croaked a warning and Corax swept towards the far side of the valley, out of the territory of his parents.

He flew to Foel Ddu and landed on a promontory of rock. The side of the mountain, blasted by quarrying, was stepped into granite terraces. From his vantage point, Corax could look across to Craig-y-Cigfran, a mountain that had hardly changed since the last ice age. Vara and Kra still circled above it, visible to Corax's keen eyes and he instinctively felt tempted to fly towards them. But the hostility of Vara was still with him and, lifting off, he veered north, along the valley over terrain he had never seen before.

The valley was some three miles long. At the southern end was Carfan village, while the valley land itself was split up into numerous small farms. Down the centre ran the road with the river known as the Afon Carfan winding close alongside. On either side, the fields were contained by dry-

stone walls. Confined by these were herds of Welsh black
cattle, their dark shapes and long, cream, black-tipped horns
attracting the young raven's eye and bringing him lower to
investigate. He glided over them, circling once to satisfy his
curiosity, then on, above the neighbouring field where the
small, brown-legged mountain sheep were grazing, un-
concerned. Many of the sheep had leapt the walls and were
browsing on the rocky, scree-clad slopes at the foot of the
mountains. Occasionally Corax would see a shepherd, with a
black-and-white collie, moving among the rocks to round up
sheep that had wandered too far.

Corax flew low now, looking for food. Not used to sheep or
cattle, he was wary of landing among them even though he
could see many other birds had done so: magpies and crows,
pigeons, starlings, peewits and sparrows, herring and black-
headed gulls, all these walked nonchalantly amid the animals,
often under their bellies as they grazed. Yet he glided past,
unsure, and missed the pickings of insects and grain and the
occasional dead rodent or young sheep, and flew on instead
to the far end of the valley. Past the eastern gap of Bwlch-y-
Maen he went, on and on, following the winding course of the
river, Nant Ddu, as it threaded between the crags, until the
distant rippling gleam of Llyn Hewel drew him down.

He knew before he landed that this was a more promising
spot. Llyn Hewel was a natural lake that had been enlarged to
become a reservoir. The shore and surface of the lake were
alive with birds of all kinds. There were even ravens there,
among the gulls and jackdaws and the coots and mallards and
the long-legged waders. Down, down he spiralled, avoiding
other birds because he was unaccustomed to their company,
and at last he settled on a stony bank. Below him, at the
water's edge, a score of birds were feeding on the mudflat.

Corax hopped diffidently on a zigzag route towards them.
They took no notice. Gaining confidence, he hopped on to

the mud and immediately snatched and gulped down a wriggling worm. His search took him in among the other feeding birds and for the next hour he fed on a variety of worms and insects, freshwater mussels which he crushed and opened, and even a dead roach which he found among the weedy shallows.

The shout of a man across the water from the pine-clad bank opposite sent the feeding birds up in alarm, Corax among them. The species segregated and the peewit flock circled, calling plaintively. Corax found himself in a group of yearling ravens like himself; among them, though he did not know it, were his brother and sister chicks. The small flock flew to the crag above the road that edged the lake and came to rest. Corax, his hunger appeased, sat among them, preening himself.

The ravens stayed there, basking in the midday sun for several hours. Then, as one, they took off, flying over rocky, bracken-clad slopes to a hillside farm where a wall-enclosed field harboured a flock of grazing sheep. There the birds landed, this time with Corax among them, and he mingled unafraid with the sheep, snatching at the grubs and insects disturbed by their grazing.

As Corax neared a patch of brambles, there was a sudden disturbance: an animal squeal and the shrill, savage squawk of a raven. Corax flew up in alarm but almost immediately descended with the other birds to investigate. A young rabbit lay dead beneath the claws of a raven. The bird, tearing at the fur, sheared off strips of flesh but had to drop them to prevent other birds grabbing the carcass. It was a losing battle and the bird managed to gulp down only a few morsels before another raven snatched the spoils away from him. The bird lunged aggressively but four or five ravens were already tearing the rabbit apart. Corax was one of them and it was his most substantial meal that day. He was bigger than most of the other birds, for his easy life in the village and the plentiful food had made him plump and heavy. Buffeting and lunging at the other birds, he found he was able to snatch the prime pickings for himself. When he hopped away, it was because he was sated and there was little left of the carcass but shreds of fur and splinters of bone.

The ravens continued feeding in the field. Corax glimpsed a rabbit moving in the briars but it disappeared down a hole when he approached. It was early evening when the birds rose and circled, calling harshly. The flock comprised ten ravens, along with half a dozen jackdaws and a pair of young magpies, but as they circled the birds divided and only the ravens flew towards the mountains.

There were only two adults in the group, distinguished from the young birds by their blacker, brighter plumage. The browner young were this year's birds and some from the year before, still not yet mature enough to breed. All had been driven by parent birds into compulsory independence and they fed and roosted communally. Corax stayed with them as they flew purposefully between the boulder-strewn, bracken-covered slopes. Only when they reached their destination did Corax recognise the landscape, for the flock was circling above a cluster of Scots pines at the end of Carfan valley. The trees, planted two centuries ago to signpost the now vanished inn on the drovers' road, stood beside the ancient trackway leading into Bwlch-y-Maen.

One by one, the birds began to settle, perching either in the trees or on the rocky ledges close behind them where the cliff was streaked with droppings. Corax circled with the others but flew off a short distance to a crag where he landed and began to preen himself. By now the sky was darkening and the shadows stole rapidly between the peaks, filling the ravines and hollows. The chorus of quiet raven croaks eventually ceased and Corax settled down for his first night in the wild.

7. *Dinas Bran*

For several weeks, Corax kept company with his own kind, adjusting to the new way of life, adapting to the daily routine of the small flock. He revelled in the freedom and in his powers of flight. Few birds can equal the aerobatic skills of the raven and Corax made the most of his mastery, soaring and swooping, rolling and diving, stalling and tumbling with such finely controlled exuberance that a shepherd on the hillside who was used to seeing such spectacles, stopped and watched with awe.

Corax learned another vital skill, too: how to kill. His first victim was a young rabbit, caught grazing too far from the cover of the brambles. The shadow of the raven sent him running across the open field. Corax followed easily and pounced, bowling the animal over. Before it could right itself, Corax had pinned it with his claws and his great bill, like a hammer, shattered its skull. The beak then became shears, severing the corpse into sections which he swallowed with huge gulps. From that moment on, Corax equalled the rest of his kind in predatory skills.

The flock gradually increased in size. Since ravens do not normally breed until their third year, more non-breeding

51

adults joined them as well as young birds driven out that summer to fend for themselves. Though the flock stayed together, Corax always displayed independence. At night, he roosted apart, though within sound of them, and frequently during the day he would leave them at the lakeside and fly off to explore for himself. In this way, he discovered the gardens and smallholdings where farmers eked out their livelihood from the small hill farms. There, he fed on fruit from the orchards, on grain from the fields, even on feed put out for the chickens. From the rubbish heaps behind the houses he became adept at finding food; and from the compost heaps, the dustbins and the kitchen gardens.

It was on one of these excursions from Llyn Hewel, where the raven flock went regularly for their first daily feed, that Corax revisited the valley of his birth.

He flew high, hundreds of metres above the top of Elidi

Fawr, the highest peak, and let the strong winds carry him. It was August and the sun was strong, creating warm air currents which he used to take him until he was over the valley. Then he descended in a slow spiral, sighting the circling shape of Kra before the old raven saw him. Corax kept his distance, avoiding the older bird's territory, and soon his keen eye picked out the familiar garden behind the house along Carfan's main street.

He continued his descent. Behind him, Kra was following, more casual and inquisitive than hostile.

There was a movement in the garden. A small dog was tethered at the back of the house, by the open kitchen door. Corax glided and landed silently on the low wall.

The dog, a young collie bitch, stood watching him. Her tail was wagging. Corax hopped down to the grass. The puppy bounded towards him, yapping, but was pulled up short by the rope tethering her to the drainpipe.

Corax hopped obliquely across the garden, approaching the dog. He arrived at the place where the dog was at the limit of her freedom and stood there, inches away from the dog's questing nose. Curious and eager to play, the puppy reared against the tether, yapping in frustration as Corax kept just out of reach.

It was the start of a teasing routine that Corax was to refine over the course of time. The puppy, after having her tail tweaked a few times, began to treat it as a game, retreating and trying to entice Corax within reach of her tether, but the raven never advanced further than one hop from safety.

From the wall behind, Kra watched impassively. The play continued until someone came to the house, walking towards the garden down the side path. It was a man, carrying a small sack. He stopped and stared at the sight of two ravens rising without panic from the garden, leaving the puppy leaping and barking in a frenzy of frustration.

The man did a strange thing. He whistled, a curious, warbling whistle. And he called out. "Blackie boy, hello, Blackie. Hello boy."

Corax flew off unhurriedly, but Kra wheeled and came back low over the garden and the man. He croaked as he passed overhead and the man kept calling: "Blackie, hello Blackie, hello Blackie boy."

Kra soared and uttered a gutteral "Blackie" as he went but the wind carried the sound and the man did not hear it. Tom Davis, now on friendly terms with the Rees family, watched and wondered as the bird flew towards the mountains and disappeared from his sight. When he took the potatoes he had brought from his garden into the house, he told Geraint's mother what he had seen.

Kra returned to Craig-y-Cigfran croaking the words he had not heard spoken to him for so long. His utterances had the precise cadence and timbre of the voice he had just heard, the voice that had taught him the words in the first place. He called them ceaselessly for the rest of the day.

Corax, meanwhile, had risen high again above the peaks, never wearying of the freedom of flight, pitching and rolling, corkscrewing, even somersaulting, as he swept past the towering crags on a course that took him back to Llyn Hewel. There, he rejoined the ravens and the jackdaws on the shore where he stayed till nightfall.

At dusk, the ravens flew to a different roost. The flock had outgrown the tree roost and this evening none of the birds settled there. Instead, with one accord, they circled and flew through the pass and along the narrow valley which a glacier had gouged out of the rock at the time of the last ice age. This access through the mountains had been used by men since the earliest times, from the first nomadic families of primitive Man to the later tribes which settled there. These tribes had in their turn been invaded by the Romans and the area was steeped in the blood of many battles. The ravens, themselves descended from the birds that had circled over marching columns and battlefields strewn with dead, hovered now above the ruins of a castle.

Erected in the eleventh century, Dinas Bran had been raised on the site of a much earlier fortification, an auxiliary Roman fort built to protect the route that led from Segontium on the coast to the city of Deva to the east; the same route was later adopted by the drovers for their cattle drives. The ravens, Corax among them, found the castle ruins to their liking as a roost and, after circling a few times, descended.

A colony of jackdaws rose at their approach, protesting harshly at the invasion. But the larger birds ignored them and found individual roosting places in the ivy-covered crevices among the tumbled masonry of towers and ramparts. The site commanded a view of most of the valley's length, and beside the river, the smooth trackway of the ancient armies glinted in the moon's light. Corax, from his ledge on a crumbling wall, croaked loudly and the bygone centuries caught the sound and sent back diminishing echoes until it faded to oblivion.

The raven flock adopted the ruins as their winter roost. The jackdaws continued to share it, though the species kept apart. As autumn stripped the leaves from the rowans and the blackthorns and the first winter winds began to whistle through the mountain gulleys, the flock increased to thirty birds. Corax would frequently fly off independently, seeking out human habitations where experience had taught he would be likely to find food.

By now, Corax had lost almost all his fledgeling traits. His dove-grey iris had become the glittering black eye of the adult. His wing coverts were still brown and his plumage had not yet developed an adult's lustrous sheen, but his chin was a

55

glossy green and his legs had darkened to black. His massive bill, curved at the top, was covered with distinctive bristles and his tail had developed the characteristic rounded, graduated shape. He had also grown the pointed, hackle-like throat feathers which, like those above his eyes, he could raise at will. His body had reached full size so that no bird likely to be found amid the surrounding mountains, save an occasional wandering great black-backed gull, could match him for weight and size. And none could match him for his powers of flight.

It was on a morning near the turn of the year, when winds from the north were chilling the mist-damped peaks to ice and Corax was indulging his flighting skills in the blustery air, that he found himself once again within sight of Craig-y-Cigfran. He plummeted past the peak, seeing no sign of Kra or Vara, and circled high above the familiar village street of Carfan. Lower and lower he came until he finally landed on the garden wall.

An almost full-size border collie bounded, barking, towards him. Suddenly, the dog stopped short and ceased barking. She remembered the huge black bird, so silent and unafraid and unlike any other that visited the garden. She bounded backwards, tail wagging, yapping playfully.

Corax hopped down to the frost-hardened ground. The dog scampered up to him, leaping at the last moment and Corax, hopping sideways, lunged and tweaked the tail. Barking with excitement, the dog repeated the same manoeuvre. Again Corax nipped her, without force, and again the dog turned so that the play could go on.

Now Corax spotted something on the grass. It was a lamb-bone, tossed there for the dog. Corax hopped to it and picked it up. The dog rushed to reclaim it but Corax danced just out of reach. Racing after him, the dog made leap after leap and each time the raven side-stepped with consummate ease.

56

Finally, panting from the exertions, the dog crouched on her haunches, face flat to the ground, and waited.

Corax hopped to the dog and dropped the bone inches from her nose. Then he jumped on to her back and tugged the wagging tail with his beak. The dog, exhausted, suffered the indignity until too severe a tweak brought her sharply to her feet. Corax flew to the shed roof, paused and then took off. Only then did Corax become aware that Kra was gliding just above him. The two ravens stooped in mock attack, without aggression, as they passed each other and then together flew off above the village.

They flew in a wide circle, calling as they went. Kra felt no need to chase off the newcomer, for this was not his territory. Something always drew him to this bird and to the village. They flew above the houses and the outlying fields and cottages. From the path leading to a woodshed near an orchard, a man, cradling a pyramid of chopped wood, stared up as they passed. He gave a singular whistle, then called.

"Hello Blackie, hello boy, hello Blackie boy."

Kra veered away from Corax and swooped down over the man. He gave a harsh croak, turned and swooped again. This time, he managed to repeat the cry he knew. "Blackie . . . ki . . . ki . . . boy. Blackie . . . ki . . . ki . . ." and he was off into the grey sky after Corax. Below, the man, who had dropped his load of wood, stared after him.

8. Survival

As winter fastened its hold on much of the ravens' food, so the hunting range of the flock increased. It was nothing now for Corax to cover ten, fifteen, twenty miles in the search. The lake shores froze, and the frosts hardened the fields and farmyard middens. Near the big town on the coast, the municipal rubbish tip, which was added to each day, attracted foraging birds from far around. The ravens were outnumbered by screaming black-headed and herring gulls, but once one of the big, black birds had seized a titbit in its beak, no bird of any other kind would attempt to take it. Corax himself flew at a lesser black-backed gull and harried it until it dropped a scrap of meat which Corax snatched and swallowed. The gull lunged and hissed but made no move to attack, even though it almost matched him in size. Encouraged, Corax flew at other gulls, frequently causing them to disgorge in fright, to the hungry raven's instant advantage.

The tip attracted other scavengers. Rats, driven by hunger from the dockside and the derelict houses, found their way to the site and scurried and dug beneath the extensive mound of refuse. Corax found them easy prey. His keen eyes spotted the exits and entrances of the runs beneath the surface and, watching the rodents enter, he would fly-hop to the hole from which he knew the rat would emerge and wait there, silent and keen-eared. His stabbing bill never missed. This stratagem almost proved his downfall, for a fox, as cunning and intelligent in its way as was the raven, was watching Corax. Knowing the bird was waiting for a rat to emerge, the animal stalked up behind, and only Corax's quick hearing saved him. As it was, the fox's snapping jaws snagged tufts from his tail feathers, which the creature spat out in disgust. The lesson was a priceless one for Corax; from then on, he was always on his guard.

The year turned and the snows came. With the snows came the winds and life became a struggle. Corax was spurred to revisit his earlier haunts. He flew along the valley towards the village. As he passed Craig-y-Cigfran, Kra and Vara paused in their frenzied courtship aerobatics and came winging out to inspect him. Corax kept his distance and neither bird harried him, returning after swooping past him to their ritual flights above the snow-capped crags. Kra's flighting antics were more subdued than usual, for his maleness and courting fervour were on the wane with age. Moments later he flew off, leaving Vara, and, curious as ever, trailed behind Corax to the village.

In the garden, the dog was now housed in a kennel. As Corax landed on the wall, she leapt towards him, but this time she was short-tethered by a chain. Corax hopped across the snow-clad grass leaving a zigzag trail of footprints. The dog crouched, whining with frustration, her tail sweeping the snow. Corax made no attempt to play. Instead, he flew up to the shed, and from there to the roof of the house. It was midday but the wind, still bringing sleet, was keeping all but a few people inside their houses. He flew from house-top to house-top. A flock of starlings and sparrows flew up from a bird-table in a garden where bread and scraps had been put out. The householder, watching from the window, blinked in amazement as a giant black bird landed on the table and lifted off with half a stale loaf in its beak.

The bread was heavy, even for Corax, and he flew labouringly back to the dog. She had returned to the warmth of the kennel but emerged barking as the bird settled. Corax hopped forward and deposited the bread.

The back door opened and the bird rose hurriedly. A boy's voice called and Corax circled, for the voice was familiar. But he did not land again and ascended to rejoin Kra who was high above the village. The boy stooped and picked up the bread. It weighed almost a pound and the dog had already started to nibble it. Looking up, Geraint glimpsed the two ravens as they disappeared. He returned indoors scarcely able to believe what he had witnessed.

Corax, meanwhile, was following Kra. The old bird, who

often came back to the place where he had heard his past calling him again, flew towards the cottage by the ancient earthworks. Snow covered the mound and the orchard trees and there was no sign of movement except on and around the crudely-made bird-table beside the house. There, tits and starlings squabbled for the scraps that Kra always found whenever he came. While Corax circled, uncertain, Kra descended, scattering the birds, and greedily snatched and gobbled down the meat and bread and vegetable scraps. His crop full, he rose, unseen by the man who was dozing by his fireside. Corax croaked with frustration, for Kra had left nothing. He followed the old bird back across the fields and rooftops of the village and along the valley. When Kra veered towards Craig-y-Cigfran, Corax continued steadily on towards the valley's end.

As he flew, Corax spotted movements in the corner of a field, near a low stone wall. Rabbits were scratching in the snow to graze. He landed behind a wall and cautiously hopped to the nearest gap, a five-bar gate, through which he gazed for a long time. Eventually, moving slowly, hopping one step at a time, he advanced in his usual zigzag fashion towards the unsuspecting rabbits. They paused frequently in their foraging, bolt upright with ears erect, but Corax continued on his sideways progress, seemingly interested in everything but them. In this way he advanced right into their midst. When he was several lengths from one young rabbit, he stayed motionless, letting the browsing creature move towards him. Too late, the rabbit realised the bird's intention as Corax slowly spread his wings. The animal leapt and ran for cover, but there was no cover near enough and the shrill squeal was cut short by a single beak-blow that scattered blood on the surrounding snow.

When his crop was filled by the flesh of the rabbit, Corax flew to the wall and preened his bloodied feathers. He stayed there half an hour, digesting his meal, then lifting off he continued up the valley. At Bwlch-y-Maen he circled, undecided whether to head for Llyn Hewel or to follow the Nant Goch to Dinas Bran. As it was mid-afternoon and already the light was going, he headed into the pass towards the roost. By the time he reached the castle ruins, snow was falling thickly. He found the raven flock already there. Two birds came out towards him, calling, but on recognising Corax they turned and the three birds winged through the driving snow to the shelter of a turret ledge. There, protected and well fed, he preened his snow-wet wing feathers, *pruking* softly with contentment.

The snow persisted, freezing overnight, and next day the land lay white and brittle. At first light the ravens lifted from the ruins, spiralling upwards and filling the narrow valley with their harsh, discordant calls. Along with jackdaws and a group of hooded crows, the flock set off towards Llyn Hewel. Corax lagged behind. Experience was teaching him that food was easier to find nearer the homes of humans; those most familiar to him lay in Carfan village, so once again, as the calls of the raven flock faded into the distance, Corax turned above the Scots pines at the opening of the pass and headed up the valley above the ice-fringed river.

He passed the towering white-clad peak of Craig-y-Cigfran but there was no sign of any other raven. Corax winged his way towards the village. In the early sun the winding stream below him glinted golden between ice-encrusted banks. From the distant village the only signs of life were the drifting curls of smoke from chimneys and the sounds of barking dogs from gardens where they stretched themselves and greeted the new day.

From above the houses, Corax had begun his slow descent to the familiar garden shed when a movement caught his attention. High above him, on the far side of the village, was another circling raven. Even at that distance, Corax could recognise Kra. Remembering the scraps the adult bird had led him to the previous day, Corax ceased his descent and flew towards him. The other bird spiralled down above the cottage and the orchard. A warning croak greeted Corax as he approached. Heeding the warning, Corax hovered, balancing on the wind, as Kra descended to the house.

The old bird landed on the apple tree nearest to the cottage, causing a deluge of snow to cascade from the branches, and uttered another call. The door opened and a man came out, carrying a plate. He crossed to the bird-table and tipped a pile of scraps on to it. The man backed away and Corax watched the other bird hop down to the table. Clearly, the routine was familiar to man and bird. From the cottage doorway, the man scattered more scraps on the ground, in the snow around his feet, all the while keeping up a constant one-sided conversation.

"Blackie, hello Blackie boy, hello Blackie."

Kra ceased feeding and turned this way and that, watching the man. But he did not fly down. Instead, he finished the scraps on the table and took off. The man watched him rise and, for the first time, became aware of Corax, drifting above the orchard. As Kra winged past him, Corax descended, landing on the ground beyond the table. The man waited. Corax stayed where he was, his head movement betraying the fact that he was watching the man. At last, realising the raven was not going to approach as long as he was there, the man went inside and closed the door. Immediately, Corax hopped to the doorway and devoured the scraps, watched by the man from the window. The last meat-bone, however, Corax did not stop to pick clean. Instead, he picked it up in his beak and took off with it. The man saw him cross the orchard and disappear towards the village.

Corax flew directly to the house he knew so well. He settled on the shed and, at once, the dog came bounding towards him, pulling up at the check of the tether. Corax hopped down to the rockery, then zigzagged across the snow until he was almost touching the straining dog's nose. He dropped the bone. The dog became frantic, for the bone was just out of reach. Corax picked it up, hopped nearer and let it fall again. This time, the dog snatched it up as Corax flew back up to the shed. Corax, head turning, watched the dog crunching the bone greedily, then lifted off. He circled above the house and the white, silent village, then headed back up the valley, the snow shining with a dazzling brightness as the rising sun's rays caught it.

The cold spell ended. The last lingering pocket of snow had vanished from the valley by the middle of February. From that moment on, spring pushed forward with no more hindrance. Pale primroses blinked from the hollows and the white spikes of blackthorn punctuated the scree-covered hillsides. On the valley farms, the first ewes began to drop their lambs.

At Dinas Bran, the raven flock diminished. Many of the birds, entering their third year, had paired off and departed, seeking a territory and nest-site of their own. Others were in the throes of courtship and would be leaving soon. The few birds that remained with Corax were second-year birds like himself, not mature enough for breeding; there were also two adult females who had lost their mates and not found replacements.

It was Corax who was the first to discover the detritus of lambing. In the fields around the farmhouses, as February turned to March, the hardy Welsh Mountain sheep were giving birth. Farmers and shepherds attended difficult births, but in the acres of boulder-strewn land that were latticed with gulleys and hollows, the small, brown-faced ewes were dropping lambs, leaving the placentas where they lay. To Corax, a scavenger by nature, such pickings were not to be missed. The others of his kind soon discovered the easy food source and by feeding from it, rid the landscape of much rotting offal. Stillborn lambs, that would otherwise have become the breeding ground for flies or have attracted vermin such as rats, were just as efficiently cleared. Hill foxes helped the birds in their task. Occasionally, a weakling, ailing and due to die, became a target for the fox or even for the ravens, and the natural outcome was accelerated.

It was towards the end of lambing time, when few ewes remained pregnant, that Corax learned to fear Man. A ewe had given birth to two lambs. The first, quickly shedding the membrane, was already staggering to its feet, its tail wagging as the mother's rough tongue licked the mucus from its face. The second lamb lay dead, stillborn. Corax, together with an adult raven, glided down as the ewe, giving up her attempt to bunt the dead creature to life with her curling horns, moved away to tend to the living. The adult raven was Vara, the mother of Corax, though this fact of nature signified nothing to either bird. Seeking food for her newly-hatched brood, she landed on the corpse and began tearing at the flesh. Corax landed a metre away, hesitant, anticipating being driven off by the older bird. As he hopped across the stony ground, there was a loud report that sent him up in a panic. In front of him, the adult raven died instantly in a thudding burst of feathers and blood and splintered bone as shots tore through the body. Corax, instinct taking over, ceased his ascent and instead dived for cover in a flight so fast that when the second shot came he was beyond the rise of the sloping ground. He continued flying low until he was safely behind a tall crag.

The farmer arrived at the corpse of the raven, spread across the dead lamb. He kicked it with disgust.

"That's one less of you black eye-gouging devils," he said. Like most sheep farmers in the valley, he felt a hatred for the bird that did such things, paying no heed that they were done to the dead. Nor did the heat of this hatred cool sufficiently to let him see the good the birds did, ridding his land of putrefying corpses which, if left, could carry disease to the living and the healthy. He looked around for Corax, angry that his second shot had missed.

It had not missed by much. Had he not dived instead of continuing to soar, Corax would have been struck by the shots that whined past his head. Swerving as he flew, he skimmed the boulders, settling only when a massive outcrop of rock separated him from the man.

He did not stay long; he was too disturbed. His instincts warned him always of natural dangers, but for this threat, the closest he had ever been to death, he had had no instinctive feeling. A wild raven has a natural wariness of Man; Corax, because of the exceptional circumstances of his early fledgeling days, had never regarded humans as dangerous. Now he knew better and never again would he approach them without caution.

Still agitated, he lifted from the rock and flew further from the scene, rising as he went until the man was a speck on the landscape. Soon, he was above Rhinog Fach, with Carfan and Nant Goch and the ruins of Dinas Bran left far behind. On he flew, further than he had ever flown, and the landscape changed beneath him from bare granite rock to dark forest, broken by frequent lakes and valleys, villages and roads. Eventually, a whole new world stretched below him with not a mountain in sight, only flat, lush fields, woods and spinneys bright with the new season's growth. Beyond lay a smoke-hazed town that pounded with life and ceaseless movement.

9. *The Visit*

Corax circled high above the busy market town, viewing this strange new world warily. Although it was similar in some ways to the village he knew, his recent narrow escape made him cautious. After soaring for an hour and more above the town's centre and the outlying houses and gardens, he drifted away from the built-up area to the open country, drawn by the flocks of rooks and gulls he could see following the plough in the surrounding fields. He glided above them, over a tractor pulling a harrow across a field previously ploughed. Corax descended and came to rest on the soil behind the busily feeding birds.

He found an abundance of food. The newly turned earth left all kinds of insects exposed and he stayed among the other birds, picking and feeding on larvae and grubs until a man stepped down from the tractor.

The birds rose and settled almost immediately but Corax took off in alarm, flying to the other side of the hedge. A movement there in the grass on the bank of the ditch which ran along the hedge caught his eye. A quick hop and he snatched up a frog, the first he had found. Devouring it

swiftly, he spotted another, and another. The ditch was alive
with them for they were heading for a nearby pond to spawn.
Globules of spawn glistened already in the shallow water of
the ditch itself. Corax attempted to eat it, but the gelatinous
mass was too slippery and unappetising. A short distance
away a magpie landed, also attracted by the frogs. Corax
lunged aggressively but the other bird stood its ground,
chattering with annoyance. Corax ignored him, snatched and
gulped another frog, then lifted off. He headed for the small
copse where ash and alder and hawthorn trees offered cover,
though many of the leaves were still clenched, awaiting
warmer days.

Corax settled in the top of an alder and the slender
branches bowed under his weight. He clung uncomfortably
for a few moments then took off, winging his way back
towards the town. The sun was sinking now and soon he
would need somewhere to roost. Meanwhile, he continued
hunting. Although his nervousness of Man made him wary of
going too close, he knew that food was to be found close to
the houses. He soared above the rooftops and gardens on the
outskirts of the town, looking for a tell-tale sign.

And there it was: a small flock of starlings feeding on the
newly dug vegetable plot at the end of a garden. He spiralled
down and landed in their midst. They kept their distance
from the giant intruder but carried on feeding. Corax fed in
desultory fashion on beetles and larvae. A dog barked from
the house some distance away, prompting Corax to fly to an
apple tree. A poodle stood on the lawn, yapping, and Corax
winged towards it. The dog, surprised by the sight of the
largest bird it had ever seen heading towards it, ceased
barking. As Corax came down to land, his outstretched
wings, twice the length of the dog, overshadowed it. The
dog's nerve broke and with shrill yelps of fear it turned and
raced for safety to the nearby shed.

The dog's cries brought its mistress to the back window. She arrived in time to see a giant black bird plucking plastic clothes-pegs from the bag hanging on the post of the washing-line and hurling them in all directions. When the bag was almost empty and the lawn and flowerbeds strewn with multicoloured pegs, Corax took a liking to a bright red one and flew off with it in his beak. He flew back to the apple tree and jammed the peg in a crevice in a high, dead branch, where it remained to puzzle the apple-pickers later in the year.

The woman emerged from the house and Corax took off quickly, veering this way and that as he went. He made his way towards a tall church tower and as he neared it, the metal weathercock on the mast-head, swinging listlessly in the wind, creaked loudly on a rusty iron pivot. Corax answered with a croak that mimicked it exactly. Again the cockerel called and again and again Corax answered. A pigeon flew from behind a gargoyle at the corner of the castellated tower and Corax dropped to investigate. A second pigeon hurriedly vacated the crevice and the raven stooped in mock attack,

chasing the bird until it found refuge in the thick foliage of the churchyard yew below.

Corax returned to the gargoyle. Behind it, where the leaded roof sloped to form a channel for the rain, a buttress created an alcove in which generations of pigeons had roosted and nested. It was large enough to admit Corax, and scratching aside the debris of droppings and twigs and feathers, he took possession of the shelter. When the two pigeons returned in the twilight they were greeted by a belligerent *korronk* that sent them veering off to seek another roost. Corax waddled to the edge of his vantage point, looking out over the night-shrouded rooftops. He uttered one last harsh call that caught the ears of the curate crossing the churchyard to his house. Though Corax could see his pale face, staring upwards in puzzlement, the man could see nothing, for the raven was as black as the shadow it occupied. Retreating into the alcove, Corax settled for the night.

It was Saturday and Geraint set out for Old Tom's cottage. Every weekend now, the boy took a bag of home-baked cakes to the man whom the Rees family had befriended. Geraint enjoyed the visits, for quite often he would see the raven that the man was wooing back to friendship. Every day Old Tom would put food out for Kra. But the bird's visits were spasmodic. Two weeks could pass before, suddenly, he was there, outside the window, gobbling down the meat and vegetable scraps which otherwise were enjoyed by starlings, magpies, jays and sparrows. When such a visit occurred, Geraint would hear all about it and perhaps even see the bird himself as he came along the road.

He turned the corner by the Carfan Arms, looking about him. The March sky glowered bleakly behind the dark rise of the ancient earthworks and gulls wheeled above the cottage.

A crow winged from a green-budded ash tree and Geraint mistook it for the raven. But the smaller size and faster wingbeats identified it and Geraint lost interest. As he passed the field, peewits rose with plaintive calls.

He reached the gateway of the path leading to the cottage. The great black shape of the raven rose and flew to the earthwork, settling on the top to watch the boy as he approached.

The door opened and Old Tom came out.

"Saw you down the road, boy. It's visiting day today, all right, isn't it?" The man was smiling, pleased.

Geraint nodded. "Yes, I've just seen Blackie. He's there, look, on the old fort."

The man came further up the path and stood by Geraint, where he could see the bird's silhouette on the mound, small and hunched and blacker than the sky behind.

"It's strange, but he's been here since first light today, as though he wants my company again." He gazed for a moment. "Like a vulture, isn't he, stood there? He's at home on that old fort, boy. His ancestors perched on the walls of that fort, waiting like a row of vultures when a battle was raging. Waiting for the dead, for the horses and men alike, I dare say."

"Were battles fought here, then?" Geraint handed the man the bag he had brought.

The man looked inside, lifted out the sausage rolls and fruit cake and replaced them.

"You thank your mam, now, boy, do you hear? Don't forget now. What's that you say? Battles fought here? Aye, boy, there were battles fought, bloody battles they were, too, such as you nor me can picture. Why else do you think the fort was built?"

"But who was fighting, Old Tom? Was it the Romans again?" Geraint recalled his school lessons on local history.

"Who else, boy? We, that is, the native tribes who held the land, the Welsh with the mountains and the streams and the valleys in their very souls, were invaded by the Romans, see. They came up from the south, from Caerleon, marching north, following the valleys and the rivers, up through this very valley. But all the time they had to fight the various tribes, see."

"I know that, Old Tom. At school, we learn the history; the Silures were in the south and the Ordovices lived up here, in the north."

"That's right, boy. The Ordovices of Powys, that is what we were called in those days. I don't know the names of any others. And we built this fortified camp, see, and others like it, to hold against the Romans."

The man broke off. "Look there, boy, old Blackie, watching us, like an old sentry, he is."

The two gazed at the bird and as they watched they saw the black shape lunge forward and the wind brought the distant harsh cry to their ears.

The man looked at Geraint. "Don't you hear it, boy? Don't you hear the past when it talks?"

As he spoke, he moved into the orchard. Geraint kept pace with him.

"I hear it often, when I'm walking over the fort, with old Blackie there. I feel it, too, so close sometimes; as though the battles and the marches took place only yesterday. I see the camp, not a heap of earth but great banks of soil and stones, and my ancestors clad in animal skins with their savage painted faces fighting to the death against the swords and javelins of the Romans, who had their shields and their armour to protect them. Trained they were, see, trained to perfection, and the tribes had nothing but their courage. Ah, we fought all right, with men like Caradoc to lead us, and we slew them, but they beat us in the end and took our forts and

72

built their own, too, and they held them for centuries."

They emerged from the orchard and began climbing the slope of the lower, outer ring of earth surrounding the mound. Ahead of them, the black bird lifted off and the deep *korronk* carried to them.

The man halted, watching the circling bird. "He knows, boy. He knows what there is, here, underneath our feet and in the air about us. His ancestors were here, with mine and yours, keeping company with Time. A special bird, he is, the raven. Linked himself earlier and closer with Man than any other bird, and here he is, still with us, see."

The bird ascended, spiralling, his calls audible but growing fainter.

"How long has he been with Man, then?" Geraint asked.

"Not just with him, boy, but part of him, see. A part of his good and a part of his evil. He's been that since the early Dawn. In the Old Testament he is, time and again, remember? Setting an example to Cain in his evil; sent out by Noah from the ark; bringing food to the prophet Elijah."

"The Romans looked on ravens as prophets," put in Geraint, remembering another lesson.

"Aye, an oracle to the Romans, was old Blackie's kin. Prophets of doom, they used to think. There are some that still do. Can you not feel it now, boy, up here, on the old camp with the bird above you and the wind on your face, the wind from the mountains and the past?"

Geraint stood on the high promontory they had now reached, for they had been climbing as they talked, and stared about him. Before him stretched the two lines of mountain crags, shadowed from the sun by a layer of dark clouds. Between the crags lay the valley and the village. A haze of mist was moving slowly from the far end, heralding the rain. Behind the mound, the sun broke through a cloud and windows in the village glinted for a second. And it was then that Geraint realised what the difference was that had always stood between Old Tom's feelings and his own. For the glint reminded him of helmets and of armour and brought to mind the marching columns he had visualised on that never-to-be-forgotten evening, and he knew *his* past lay, not with Old Tom and the tribes, but with the ordered ranks of the invaders who had come from the shores of southern Europe.

Turning slowly, Geraint met the gaze of Old Tom burning into his, and as the single sun-ray cast the shadow of the raven overhead across them both, so all three shared a moment that had leapt from past to present; then the shadow vanished and the cloud obscured the sun and the first raindrops came in the wind. Without speaking, the two hurried down the slope towards the cottage.

10. On the Shore

Corax glided from the church tower in the early dawn. The town was still sleeping. The pale pink of a new day was nudging back the night sky from the eastern horizon and shadows were already growing as he soared above the still gardens. He let the March wind carry him high, his wing movements barely discernible, so that he could look down on the whole town and the fields around it. It seemed as though he had the world to himself, but from the hedgerows, linnets and chaffinches were already fluttering and from the house eaves, sparrows and starlings tumbled boisterously.

Corax stayed high, watching the light replace the darkness. Although he could not hear the cockerels crowing, he could see them on their morning perches going through the motions; cats hurried across the gardens to the houses where they knew they would be fed; dogs let out for their morning run raced around the gardens. Cars emerged from the drives and people from the houses as the town came to life. Descending slowly, he watched the horse-drawn cart laden with logs and chopped wood moving stop-start down the street.

He dropped to a house-top where he perched beside a television aerial, intrigued by the horse. The carter selling his wares made his to-and-fro journeys to the back door of each house, unaware of the raven's presence. Corax dropped to a garden wall near the horse, which snorted uneasily at the sight of the giant bird.

The man took a sack of logs from the cart and went off to the house. Corax hopped nearer to the horse, then flew up to the top of the cart. The horse turned its head with difficulty to watch him. Corax hopped down and stood on the horse's back. The silky, frisking tail fascinated him. He lunged and tugged at the hair.

There was a whinny of pain from the horse. Although the brake held the wheels of the cart, the horse pulling with full strength to escape the tweaking of his tail was able to move it. Snorting and whinnying as the merciless beak plucked his tail-hairs, the horse gathered speed. There was a cry from the garden and the carter came running out to see his horse and cart disappearing swiftly down the road. Calling angrily, he set off in pursuit. He saw the black bird rise as he drew near the horse but did not see where it came from. Grabbing the reins, he pulled the frightened horse to a standstill. It had covered almost a hundred metres. When he had recovered his breath, the puzzled man turned the horse and the vehicle and began to retrace his steps. As he walked, he heard the rasping clucks of the big black bird on the nearby rooftop. Beside him, the horse whinnied uneasily. But Corax had lost interest and flew off, disappearing behind the cupressus trees separating the gardens. The man calmed his restless animal and continued up the road, bewildered by the way his day had started.

Corax flew from the town to where he had found the frogs. He caught a mating pair in the ditch, the small male clasping the enormous female. Disposing of these, he crossed to the copse where he spotted a vole in the grass, injured by an owl in the night. This, too, he killed and ate.

By now, it was broad daylight and he flew high again. The streets and roads below were filling rapidly with people and traffic. Corax suddenly ceased drifting in a wide circle and flew purposefully westwards, towards the mountains whence he had come.

He flew strongly, without varying his speed and without stopping. The flat plain gave way to hills, then to rocky outcrops and plantations of pines and soon he was once again above the granite crags, the tallest of them gleaming white as the sun's rays caught the snowcaps.

He flew on, over a succession of valleys, his direction unerring. Above the ruins of Dinas Bran he circled once, then continued to Llyn Hewel. Descending, he skirted the stunted willows and the mudflat, but seeing only waders, coots and moorhens, he rose again without alighting. On he went, towards the coast, and at the rubbish tip outside the coastal town he flew down to join the other ravens.

Corax stayed with the flock until midday. When a party of a dozen ravens flew up and headed for the seashore, Corax went with them. It was his first visit to the shore. While the other birds settled on the sand left ridged and shining by the retreating tide, Corax explored the new terrain. He winged low across the sand as far as the cliffs then back again towards the sea, flying out above the surface and experiencing the salt spray lifted by the wind from the wave crests as they rolled ceaselessly on to the shore. He revelled in the sensation, stooping so that his feet skimmed the water, before soaring again. Now he rolled and tumbled for the sheer joy of it, waiting for the waves to gather, rise, curl and unfurl in a crash of spray, timing his stoop so that he caught only the finest drops of spray on his plumage.

Eventually tiring of the game, he turned his attention to the expanse of sand that stretched for several miles below granite cliffs and provided feeding grounds for a multitude of birds.

He flew at cliff-top height towards a group of ravens which his keen eyes had spotted far along the shore. He could see the carrion, too, long before he arrived: a dead grey seal, already disembowelled by the other ravens but still coated with flesh. He glided down and landed beside the corpse. Six other ravens, busy tearing at the flesh, took no notice of him, though one turned to drive away a lesser black-backed gull, as large as the raven itself. Other gulls screamed in frustration as they wheeled above the feast, not daring to land.

Corax hopped to the carcass and his powerful bill sheared through the tough seal hide as though it was paper, tearing off long strips of blubber. He fed until his crop was filled, and his flight to a ledge on the cliff was more laboured than usual. He stayed on the cliff for the rest of the day, digesting the meal, and it was not until he saw the other ravens flocking that he left his perch and flew to join them. In the thickening light, the flock flew the five miles inland to Dinas Bran where Corax found his usual sheltered roost and huddled there, preening his feathers, tasting the sea salt.

The shore, now he had discovered it, became the favourite hunting ground for Corax. He returned next day to find the seal carcass gone, washed away by the incoming tide. Instead, he hopped among the rocks, learning in a matter of minutes how to dislodge the limpets from the rocks with a sharp tap of his bill. He discovered several stranded mussels and as the tide turned and withdrew, exposing countless small pools, he caught his first crab which he smashed and then crushed before picking out the flesh. Before long, he had sampled several kinds of molluscs and even managed to snatch a sand eel wriggling in a sandy shallow. The rotting head of a large fish cast up by the waves provided a further meal and he drove away the angry gulls who had found it first with confident, aggressive lunges of his bill.

The days turned into weeks and spring to summer and Corax visited the shore most days. Other favoured grounds were the sheep farms in the valleys, where rabbits and rats abounded, and where there was an occasional dead sheep; or the water's edge of Llyn Hewel where, in among tussocks of the marshy mudflats, he found and ate the eggs of peewits, redshanks, snipe and curlew, sometimes catching the young as they either darted for cover or froze, relying in vain on

their downy coats for camouflage. He also caught and ate the young of mallard and even killed a full-grown drake, snagged and helpless in a discarded fishing line.

The summer days of routine feeding were not without incident. On a day in August, when the bay was dotted with the coloured sails of the fair-weather holiday yachtsmen, Corax was patrolling the shore just below the cliffs. A flock of swirling gulls attracted him and he headed towards them. Rising, he increased his speed and dashed into their midst, his *kruk, kruk, kruk* sounding loudly as he rolled over and over, startling the unsuspecting birds. Suddenly his call changed: *korronk*, came the loud warning croak as he turned on his back and cocked his beak at the sky. A hurtling peregrine, which only his keen eye had spotted, was distracted and missed the black-headed gull it had selected. As the birds scattered widely, the falcon changed direction towards Corax. But it veered away for the second time when the raven flicked over on his back with his beak opened in defiance. Again the falcon hurtled past and Corax even set off in pursuit, though the bird outdistanced him in seconds. Moments later, Corax resumed his aerobatic game among the gulls as they regathered.

Corax had a second confrontation a few days later, this time with a greater black-backed gull. The gull was the largest bird of the coast, although an infrequent visitor to this stretch of the shoreline. From a distance it resembled the lesser black-backed gull, which Corax knew of old put up little resistance when harassed. He had garnered many an easy meal by harrying the smaller gull into disgorging its catch for him to devour on the shore below. But this larger bird reacted differently, even though its flight was laboured owing to the heavy fish it was carrying crosswise in its bill. As Corax stooped in mock attack, he was startled to find his aggression more than matched. The huge gull came straight for him, without releasing his catch, and the bill, even bigger and more powerful than the raven's, lunged in mid air. If it had not been for masterly control of his flight by a flick of his wing, Corax would have had his breast split open. As it was, the quick roll to one side caused the gull to miss and a puff of downy black feathers drifting in the wind was the evidence of the raven's narrow escape.

Corax did not attempt a second attack. It needed only one encounter with a gull that was almost twice his weight, and whose bill dwarfed even his own, for him to learn the lesson. Instead, he directed his aggression at a wave-skimming cormorant. The luckless bird swerved but its agility was no match for the raven's and it soon disgorged its catch. The fish fell straight into the sea before Corax could snatch it and the meal was lost to both birds.

During these summer days, Corax was as likely to go off on his own as he was to keep company with the flock, which was now increasing. The year's young, driven from their nests by their parents and forced to survive on their own, had met and joined the flock just as Corax had done. The group now numbered nearly twenty birds, and as winter approached it would increase even more.

For Corax, this would be his second winter. He was by now quite fully grown and the moult through the summer had replaced all the brown feathers of immaturity with the glossy black plumage of the adult. Yet he was not truly black, for in a certain light there was an iridescence; his crown was glossed with green and his back and wings and tail had a blue and purplish sheen. Beneath his chin, the greenish gloss gave way to reddish-purple on the upper breast and a deeper bluish-purple lower down. His beak and legs were black. But it was only when the sun's rays caught him that he revealed these secret colours. To most eyes he was a bird as black as night. He was large, too, even for a male, and from his experience of Man he had learned more than other ravens, so that on the farms and round the human habitations he was the cleverest and most cunning of his clever cunning kind and the most adept at finding food.

It was in the early autumn, on a mid-September day when, for no specific reason, as he left his roost at Dinas Bran, he turned and winged towards the valley and the village. He flew in a leisurely fashion, rising high above the ground mist, and was soon within sight of the peak of Craig-y-Cigfran. He looked out for one or other of the ravens whose territory he knew this was.

But Vara was dead. Crows had long since snatched the five chicks, which had soon died without both parents to feed them. The lone raven who appeared from the mountainside as Corax passed made no attempt to harass him. It was Kra, whose great age was telling, for his flight was laboured and his croak lacked any real warning. He followed Corax towards the village.

11. The Call

Geraint turned the corner from the footpath across the heath to the main road. The street was deserted. He turned and whistled up the black-and-white collie which hurried obediently to his heels.

"Good girl, Sheba. Heel now, heel." He headed for the house. From the chapel beyond the line of parked cars at the end of the street he could hear the sound of the organ and singing. Most of the inhabitants of Carfan were giving voice to their faith as they did every Sunday, just as their parents and grandparents had done. The cars were an indication that the call of chapel devotions reached out beyond the village, out into the surrounding farmsteads. As Geraint neared his gate, he answered a wave from the window of the house opposite, from his schoolfriend Alun Poole. The younger generation of the village felt the pull of Sunday chapel less strongly than their elders. Geraint attended sometimes, but more often than not he chose to take the collie for a walk, especially on a morning that was free of mist and rain for the first time in a week. Even so, the September wind was cold, driving down the valley from the north-east, and Geraint shivered, wishing he was more warmly clad.

He turned into the gateway. At the same moment, he saw the ravens, two of them, descending to the house. He stopped and stared, incredulous. The dog beside him followed his gaze. When she spotted the birds, she broke into excited barks and ran down the side path to the garden, with Geraint hurrying behind. He had not seen Corbie since the early spring, when his amazed eyes had witnessed the presenting of half a loaf of bread to the dog that even now was barking in apprehensive recognition. Geraint watched the leading raven spiral closer and although it had the glossy blackness of an adult, he had no doubt it was Corbie. The dog ran on to the small lawn bounding up on the rockery, where she stood, tail scything the air as she barked furiously. Geraint stayed near the house and watched.

The raven landed on the shed roof. Above it, the second raven circled: *pruk, pruk, pruk*; Geraint could hear the low call as the bird passed over him at rooftop height.

Corax hopped down to the rockery from the shed. The dog

backed away, uttering quick, nervous barks though her tail was still wagging. Geraint could tell from the dog's attitude that she was ready for play, for she crouched down on her forepaws, backside in the air with her bright eyes fixed on the visitor.

The bird hopped towards her. The dog made a mock attack and the raven side-stepped, hopped over the dog and managed to tweak the tail before the dog turned to make another frontal foray. The procedure was repeated half a dozen times and it was clear that the dog was deliberately exposing herself to the playful tweak time after time. Geraint, absorbed by the game, moved forward from the side of the house without thinking. The bird, much to Geraint's disappointment, at once flew up in alarm uttering an angry *korronk*.

"Corbie, boy, come on now. You know me. Come on, Corbie."

Geraint made the clucking noises he used to make to bring the bird to feed, but to no avail. The raven was clearly nervous of him, though no truly wild bird would have stayed as close as the nearest hawthorn tree beyond the garden wall. But when Geraint continued advancing, the bird flew off again, keeping his distance. There was obviously a limit to how close he would come. Geraint turned and walked slowly back to the house. He went into the kitchen, from where he could watch through the window, and waited. He could see the bird hovering above the hawthorn and hear the insistant *pruk, pruk* call.

Corax flew above the garden, watching the dog, which was looking up, barking expectantly. Of Kra there was no sign. Corax, keeping a wary eye open for the boy, continued his slow descent and finally landed on the shed while the dog raced round in a frenzy of eagerness to play.

On the far side of the village, Kra was circling as he usually did before gliding down to the bird-table near the house, where the man usually left the food.

It was there, above the bantams which scratched around beneath it looking for any fallen scraps dislodged by the boisterous sparrows and starlings. These now flew up with a whirring of wings as Kra descended and they perched on the slate roof of the cottage, chattering angrily as the great black bird took their place on the table.

From the window, Old Tom watched the raven eating. He went to the door, opened it quietly, and stepped outside. The bird paused, cocking its head, then continued to feed. The feathers of the bird's crown were thin and straggly and bald patches were visible, for Kra's waning metabolism was no longer replacing feathers shed in the annual moult and his plumage was lack-lustre and dishevelled.

The man made friendly clucking noises.

"Hello, Blackie boy. Hello boy."

"Hello Blackie boy," said the raven, distinctly.

The man chuckled quietly, his pleasure boundless. "You're going bald and grey, Blackie, just like me."

"Hello boy," said the bird.

The man waited while the raven fed. There were still scraps left on the table when the bird spread its wings and with heavy, cumbersome strokes, lifted off and flew to the apple tree. The bird's weight bowed the branches and apples fell with gentle thuds. The orchard trees were laden, for the man did not pick the crop. He let Geraint take all he wanted to his family and the rest were due to be picked by the local grocer in a week's time. Meanwhile ripe apples were falling continuously.

The man followed the raven into the orchard. In spite of his thick, ragged sweater, he shivered in the cold air.

"We are in for a sharp winter, Blackie boy. My old bones tell me and I dare say yours are doing the same, eh?"

The bird did not move till the man was two metres away. Then it flew unhurriedly to the next tree. Behind, at the cottage, the sparrows and starlings returned to the scraps.

As the man walked, he kept up the clicking sounds with his tongue. He could hear the bird mimicking him. Soon, with the bird keeping little more than an arm's length away, the man reached the first of the grass-covered ramparts surrounding the vast mound.

He walked up the slope to the first level. His breath did not come easily and he could hear himself wheezing. From the hillock above came a breathy echo. The bird had hopped ahead of him and picked up the sound. A wry smile flitted across the man's face.

"Every picture tells a story, eh, Blackie. Don't you mock me now, boy. You don't look too bright yourself, you know."

The bird wheezed again. The man mounted the second slope. He turned to look across the village. There was still another tier to go but he waited, for his chest pained him and he needed to recover his breath. The bird flew on and the man followed slowly.

From the top, he could look out over the houses and down the length of the valley. The mountains either side and the shadowy peaks at the end stood like the jagged edges of a giant bowl. The man loved this view and each time he made the trip, he marvelled at the strategic positioning of the ancient fort. It commanded the whole valley and, in effect, was approachable only from this front. He found it easy to imagine the valley without the village: the sides more verdant and the centre filled by a wide river. Now only the shallow stream remained and apart from a scattering of gaunt, statuesque Scots pines and clumps of blackthorns and hawthorns, rowans and gorse, the sides were mostly scree;

except, that is, where the quarrymen had blasted the granite for slates and cleft the mountain sides, leaving flat, sheer scars like cauterised wounds. The scars stood black and sweaty in the pale September light and the wind picked up pockets of dust as though sent up by galloping horses. The raven called, a babbling *pruk, pruk, pruk* ending with faint, ventriloquial cries, like plaintive calls for help from far, far off.

The man sat down on the cold earth and closed his eyes. The climb had taken more out of him than he had realised. He opened them on the valley and it seemed the puffs of dust were thicker and the glint of light upon the occasional white stone staring from the dry-stone wall along the roadside conjured up an impression of the faces of hiding men. Behind, on the bracken-clad slopes before the scree, the scattered shapes of sheep looked like an army making its stealthy way towards the fort. A car passed, catching the sun like a chariot, and the soldiers in the field formed into lines, still making for the fort. The bantam cockerel called and the high primeval notes echoed, to be taken up by other cockerels. The old man blinked as the soldiers reached the lower slopes and, in the wind, the whistling of the javelins was almost but not quite drowned by the cries of the wounded and the dying. Fur-clad warriors grappled and stabbed at the glinting armoured lines which moved inexorably forwards, forcing them to withdraw to the fort. Time and time again, the retreating fur-clad men regrouped but always the armour and the impenetrable wall of shields advanced until there were more warriors in heaps upon the stony ground than there were on their feet.

And even louder than the shouts of dying men could be heard the deep, harsh croaking of the great, black birds, hovering and descending, hopping and plucking, tearing and shearing, until the sound drowned every other and filled the valley and reached in among the mountains, back, back up the gulleys and the clefts into the granite rocks whence they had come. Their echoes resounded, diminished, died. Then came one more raven's cry and the old man sat as though turned to stone, for it had come from right beside him. He turned and could have touched the great, black, dishevelled bird that stood next to his seated body. As he slowly moved, the bird hopped away and lifted off, but the cry had gone deep into the man, like the pain that had made fast its grip, and he knew it would always be with him.

Standing unsteadily, he stared at the sky. The wing-jagged bird circled once then set off up the valley, its course taking it over the village. Carefully, the man made his way down to the cottage.

Kra called as he passed above the garden. From below him, Corax rose and the dog yapped as the game abruptly ended. The boy, hearing the call, emerged from the house in time to see both birds heading for the mountains. He watched them until he could see them no more.

The two ravens flew to Craig-y-Cigfran, Kra leading the way. Approaching the mountain, the old raven slowed and Corax passed him, but Kra did not turn off and make for the ledge and huge deserted nest as he had always done before. Instead, he kept straight on, this time letting Corax lead, and the two birds flew the valley's length. Corax called a single harsh *korronk* as he veered eastwards and up the narrower defile towards the castle ruins. As they neared them, three other ravens flew towards them out of curiosity and turned and flew back with the two newcomers to the ancient roost on Dinas Bran. Kra settled a few lengths away from Corax and *pruked* softly as he preened himself. His nesting days were over, winter was approaching and it was his choice to return to the company of his own kind.

12. In Winter's Grip

The signs of a severe approaching winter continued. The swallows and house martins had all departed before September was out, and the wind from the north-east was colder than usual. Before the end of October, snow was falling on the high ground, and the peaks of Foel Ddu and Craig-y-Cigfran gleamed white in the fitful watery sun. At night, when the moon could be glimpsed through clouds, it wore the halo that presaged the next day's mist and rain; rain that by November had turned to sleet.

During these bleak autumn weeks, the raven flock established its daily feeding routine. It now numbered more than twenty birds. Kra and Corax travelled with it most days; from the roost to the shore of Llyn Hewel; from there to one or other of the sheep farms to the west; then on to the sea, timing their visits with the outgoing tide and never failing to find carrion and other food on the exposed rocks and shingle and mud.

The flock did not always stay together; several birds would fly off independently and often Corax or Kra would be with them. Sometimes the two would fly together, but more often each went alone and the destination was almost always Carfan: Corax to the garden, where the dog would greet him from the kennel; Kra to the cottage where, if scraps were not already waiting for him, they would appear when the man saw him arrive.

In the first week of December, snow fell. The blizzard lasted two days and nights and no one in the valley could remember such a fall so early. The roads were blocked and only heavy vehicles could get through. To Geraint's disappointment, these included the school bus; deliveries to the shops succeeded and tractors managed to take fodder to the sheep. Life in Carfan went on almost as normal.

For the ravens, it was a different story. Corax stayed with the flock and flew to Llyn Hewel, but the birds found little there to sustain them. The farms, too, were snowbound and unrewarding. It was only at the refuse tip outside the coastal town that, along with the many hundreds of gulls already there, Corax managed to find food.

Kra, however, did not accompany the ravens. On leaving the roost to find the land buried under a deep white mantle, the old raven headed straight away to the one place where he knew he would find food.

The blizzard was still blowing as he flew and although the distance was not far, less than five miles, the bird found the going difficult. When he eventually descended to land heavily on the apple tree nearest the cottage, he was exhausted.

Old Tom did not see the bird at first. Slowed by the cold, he sat clad in an ancient army greatcoat in front of a log fire. Beside the hearth stood a stack of logs; the smaller logs he had chopped into lengths himself, and the larger ones had been cut by Geraint, who visited the cottage most weekends.

When the man stirred from the fireplace to go and make a pot of tea, he glanced out as he always did and saw the raven. He knew at once that something was wrong. Always, when it visited him, the bird hopped from the apple tree where it landed to the table. There, if no scraps were waiting, the bird would call while hopping vigorously up and down until some were brought out. Today, the bird was silent and was still perched in the tree, hunched and motionless.

The man hurried to the door, pulling his greatcoat round him. He picked up the bag of meat and vegetable scraps that he had ready and went outside. The cold made him gasp, but he bent against the driving wind and snow and put the food on to the table. He crossed slowly to the tree.

"Come on now, Blackie boy. Feeling the cold like me, I dare say. Now you get stuck into that food there, see. Or shall I take you? Are you going to let me take you?"

The man advanced cautiously. He could see the raven's black eye on him. As a young bird, the raven had been willing to fly to his outstretched arm, like a hawk. He held out his arm as he used to. The bird, now only a metre away, edged away further, shifting its feet down the branch.

"All right, Blackie boy, I'll leave you to it. I'll go in now."

The man returned to the cottage. The cold seemed to draw the band of pain round his chest even tighter. He closed the door behind him, breathing heavily, straightening up when the pain had eased. Crossing to the window, he saw that the raven had flown straight to the table and was busily eating.

"Well, I did not expect to see you, Blackie, not today," he mused. "But I suppose I should have known. You always were the clever one. You know where to come when times are hard, eh? Where the food comes easy."

He returned to the chair by the fire and turned it so that when he sat, he could still see the table outside and the raven feeding.

It was Saturday when the blizzard ceased, though the wind remained cold and the temperature barely rose above freezing. On the road the snow lay well over ankle-deep, but at least Geraint was able to visit; to take a bag of homemade griddle cakes and bread loaves to Old Tom and perhaps to chop up some more wood.

Geraint always enjoyed the walk, even in such wintry conditions. The village had taken on a Christmas-card appearance, snow capping every house, every wall, every fence post, whitening the edge of every twig on every tree. In the fields the sheep looked a dingy brown against the snow as they stood clustered round the dumps of fodder. Only tractors could make headway on the roads, and all the cars lining the roadside had been abandoned until conditions improved.

As Geraint reached the path to the cottage, he saw the raven on the roof. It stayed, hunched, as he walked to the door, knocked and entered.

The old man was in the chair, in his long coat, as still and hunched as the bird outside. Geraint was struck by the similarity. But the man rose and came to greet him.

"Hello there, Geraint *bach*. Just the boy I wanted to see. I will be needing some more wood soon. If you could drag some in here and leave it, I will chop it as I need it, see."

Geraint put down the bag. "Here are some griddles, Old Tom, from my mam, and a couple of loaves. I will chop the wood with pleasure. Mam says you are not to do the chopping, see, not until you are properly better. Is that Blackie on the roof?"

Geraint went out into the orchard, where drifts of snow were up to his waist. The bird on the roof moved only its head, while the man stood in the doorway.

"Yes, it is. Old Blackie come home. He went away, like I did, but we are both back together now, like when we started. For good, this time, the pair of us. It is all very fitting, isn't it now?"

Geraint studied the man, puzzled. He saw the thin, drawn

face, pinched with pain, and the tremble of the hands, and felt a sudden misgiving. He could not follow the meaning of the words the man was speaking.

"Look, you go back into the warm, Old Tom; I'll chop some firewood for you. We don't want you without any if more snow comes."

As the man went in and closed the door, Geraint waded through the snow to the outhouse. Two dead apple trees had blown down in the orchard and it was these that were providing the logs. He lifted down the axe from beneath the overhang of the outhouse where it was kept, noticing the fresh bird-droppings on the wood.

"So you sleep there some nights, do you, Blackie? Well, at least you are company for him. And him for you, I dare say."

The bird on the roof cocked its head, watching his progress across the orchard to the fallen trees. Handling the axe with practised ease, Geraint hacked off lengths of wood and cut them into smaller pieces. He made several trips to the cottage with armfuls of logs. He had finished by midday, and the stack beside the fireplace was as high as the chimney opening.

"Right, Old Tom, I am going now. Are you all right for food?"

Geraint crossed to the pantry door and opened it. The shelves were well filled with tins of all kinds. Geraint's mother and father had seen to that during the weeks of autumn.

The man made to rise but Geraint restrained him.

"I will probably be in tomorrow. If not, then Mam will come the next day. Anything you want now?"

The man shook his head. "All I want, boy, all I want. Thou shalt not want. Everything I'll ever need. Love to your mam, now."

Shrugging, Geraint turned and left. The old man was not making sense today. He walked down the path, watched by the raven. At the road, he looked back, and the image of the

white-capped cottage with the hunched, black bird on the
rooftop was to remain with him.

That night, after a break of less than a day, the snow came
again. All through Sunday it continued and it had not eased
by the next day. Carfan and hundreds of small villages like it
became snowed in; no vehicles could move in or out, schools
closed, sheep and cattle were marooned, their only hope of
food and survival depending on what the farmers could get to
them; to those, at least, that had sheltered close to the stone
walls and had not become buried.

And still the snow fell, brought by unrelenting winds from
the Arctic and covering the landscape deeper than living
memory or recorded history could recall. In the valley,
channelled by winds gusting down the ravines and mountain
passes, some drifts reached a depth of ten metres. More and
more livestock was buried and froze to death. On the side of
Foel Ddu, where the quarry blasting had cracked deep into
the granite, the biting frost and the weight of snow caused
several thousand tons of rock to slip grumbling down the
hillside, destroying walls and gates and bringing down a
pylon so that, for half a dozen farms, electricity was cut off.

In Carfan, the villagers struggled to survive, pooling their
resources, trying to keep at least the main street clear. The
outlying cottages and farmsteads could not be reached and
Geraint and his family worried about Old Tom. Beyond the
village, in the hostile wilderness of wind and gusting snow,
the creatures of the wild found the struggle harder. Corax,
like many of the other ravens, abandoned routine feeding
with the flock and fed where he could, his search taking him
further and further afield each day. He kept to the coast, for
even though the snow settled on the beaches, the tides
periodically cleared it, exposing the only visible land for miles

around. Here, he managed to find sandworms and shellfish and the occasional eel or dead fish; at other times he would bully the smaller gulls into giving up their meals.

When the tide was in, however, he resorted to the coastal towns, mixing with gulls around the harbours. As the days wore on and farmers managed to reach their buried sheep, corpses were exposed, and these saved the lives of ravens as well as of many other birds, and the lives of animals too, for foxes, stoats and weasels, rats and even polecats lived on sheep carcasses while this severe winter showed no signs of abating.

Corax fed better than most other birds. Unless a greater black-backed gull had found a dead sheep first, he was the biggest and the most aggressive of the hungry predators. Punching at the softest part of the dead animal, which after the eyes was the underbelly, he would tear into the entrails and gorge till he could eat no more. Within a day of finding his first sheep corpse, he became adept at spotting the signs of a buried animal: the pouching in the surface of the snow, caused by the warm breath of the creature trapped below; or, by flying low, he could sometimes see the shape of sheep only lightly buried. On these, he would land and scratch aside the snow until, with claws and bill, he could rip away the thick wool fleece and reach the flesh.

Sometimes, a sheep was still alive, though dying, comatose with cold. To such an animal Corax gave no more quarter than any other living creature ever did in the need to stay alive. In fact, of all the birds that managed to survive, it was the raven who succeeded best. Without this great crow's skill at finding carrion, without the natural digestive ability to thrive on almost any food, from flesh and grain and insects to molluscs, fruit and seeds, the true predators – the peregrines and kestrels, the merlins and the several owls – perished in large numbers.

Indeed, the loss of bird and animal life was catastrophic. No farmer had foreseen such exceptional conditions and none escaped without a loss of livestock, not even on those farms where emergency supply-drops of fodder were made by helicopters. Too often, the bales of hay plunged into five-metre drifts of snow and served no purpose. A few sheep were spotted and dug out just in time and carried one by one to the shelter of a byre. The cattle fared better than the sheep: their height and bulk kept them visible for longer and fewer died. The desperate farmers searched by night as well as by day, but away from the farms, where people lived more communally, life was nothing like so bad. In Carfan, though all roads were blocked and no vehicle could enter the village or leave it, there were sufficient food supplies in the homes and at the two small general stores to keep the population fed and warm. In the village itself, no one suffered unduly.

On the seventh day, exactly a week after Geraint had left him with a healthy stack of logs and cakes and bread, Old Tom woke in his bed to see that the fire was almost out, even though he had piled it high the night before. He pushed back the blankets and swung his legs to the cold stone floor. He knew by the sickly yellow window light that it was day. Getting to his feet with difficulty, he moved slowly to the log pile and put on three more logs, his first act every morning. His next was to go to the door, putting on the greatcoat over the clothes in which he had slept. The blizzard was still gusting as it had without respite for six days and nights. On a paper near the door, a tin of meat, opened ready, lay beside a piece of stale cake. Pulling on his boots, he took the food outside, closing the doorlatch behind him.

He walked to the end of the cottage. To his surprise, the raven was not at its roost, under the overhang of the outhouse

97

roof where it stayed each night, protected on all sides. Looking anxiously around, he saw it on the apple tree, still and huddled against the driving snow. Without hesitating, the man plunged through the drifts, which in places reached his waist, and put the paper with the meat and cake on the snow beneath the tree. The bird's head moved as it watched him.

The man straightened up. He stood rigid as the realisation dawned, and then the pain was gone, the tight excruciating band around his chest was at long last unwinding. Black bird, bare branch, white flakes spun and flashed and faded and then there was nothing; nothing but the smile on the upturned face which the snow immediately began to shroud.

The blizzard continued unremitting for another week. And then it ceased. The food and fuel in Carfan were almost gone, but immediately work began to clear the roads. Within twenty-four hours, snowploughs had opened a way for the first deliveries to get through and the worst danger passed.

For Geraint and his family, the first task was to try and visit Old Tom in his cottage. For two weeks now, it had been impossible, the whole route buried under impassable snow. But on the fifteenth day, Geraint and his father managed to struggle to the cottage. It took them a whole morning, shovelling through the deeper drifts, but by midday they had reached the door. Geraint, whose feelings of misgiving had stayed with him, saw what he had feared. The door was hidden by a drift of snow that reached almost to the eaves. No one had passed through there for many days. His father, avoiding looking at him, began to dig into the drift. Geraint helped him clear it and the closed door was revealed. The latch opened easily and they went inside, closing the door behind them.

The fireside chair was empty. The fire was out, the hearth cold. It had been out for days. The room was ice-cold, like a tomb, the windows blocked by drifts outside so that a dim and sinister yellow light was all that penetrated. Geraint stared at the log-pile. It was lower than he had left it. Almost half the logs had been taken from it and burned. He crossed to the pantry and studied the shelves. There were a few tins less than when he had last looked. In the dustbin in the corner were empty cans and wrappers. Of Old Tom there was no sign.

The two stood looking round the room, helpless. Geraint went to the door, opened it and looked outside. The orchard, the great mound of the ancient earthwork, lay buried under impenetrable snow. At one point, only the tip of an apple tree showed. There was nothing anyone could do.

"Perhaps someone came and took him to their house, Geraint," said Mr Rees, but Geraint knew it was not so and that his father knew it, too.

He shrugged. "Best leave it now, Da," he said, stepping out through the drift they had dug. His father closed the door. In silence, they set out for the village. Geraint, glancing back at the white outline of the cottage, saw again the black, hunched bird that had been there on his last visit, and the image was so vivid that he had to blink to realise it was behind his eyes, and not before them. He followed his father, remembering what Old Tom had told him of the raven, and wondering.

13. Death and Fulfilment

The year had turned before the artic weather let up. The snow had ceased, but for days after, the frost held fast. Gradually, however, warmer winds came and the long, slow thaw began.

With the thaw came a change in the routine of Corax and the rest of the flock. Melting snow revealed the corpses of many animals, chiefly sheep, and there were scores of these. The bodies of the cows were quickly recovered by the farmers, but sheep carcasses remained undiscovered on the higher slopes among the crevices where they had vainly sought shelter. The ravens, carrion and hooded crows and buzzards as well as animal predators soon discovered them. Some farmers, wise to the ways of wildlife, were guided by the vulture-like congregations of the ravens to find the carcasses and recover them. But enough remained for the birds to feast on for many days.

Then there were the floods, for the melting snow swelled the mountain streams and the rushing water overflowed the banks and filled the hollows and spread across the valley's lower fields. Corax found the victims of a flooded warren and fed on rabbit carcasses as well as on those of drowned voles and mice.

As the land recovered and the seasonal January weather resumed, so too did the cycles of life. The ravens, always among the earliest birds to respond to the mating urge, dispersed and went their separate ways. Corax, once the snow had ceased, visited with increasing frequency Kra's territory at Craig-y-Cigfran. There was no sign of the bird. No warning croak from any raven met him when he circled near the ledge that was his birthplace. The massive nest stood empty and deserted. With Corax flew another raven from the flock. This was Rega, a female the same age as himself. At first, the two birds returned each evening to Dinas Bran to roost, but as soon as the weather improved, they began to linger in the valley when it was dusk, and finally the night came when they stayed on the ledge. From then on, the raven pair regarded the site as their own. And the courtship of Rega by Corax began.

The thaw led to the uncovering of more death. Geraint's father and two other men hurried to Tom Davis's cottage as soon as the snow allowed. Geraint was at home when his father returned, grim-faced, with the news that the body of the old man had been recovered, frozen and looking as though he had died that very day. The body had been taken to the local hospital and it seemed already certain that the cause of death would be put down as a heart attack. Hypothermia would be ruled out, Mr Rees felt, because there was sufficient food and fuel left in the cottage for many more days.

Geraint slipped out of the house quietly after hearing the news, leaving his father comforting his mother who, although like everyone else had been prepared for the discovery, was still deeply upset by it. Geraint made his way down the village

street to the corner and turned off towards the distant
earthwork, which rose like an island from the flooded fields
around it.

Geraint's heart was heavy as he made his way along the
route he had travelled so many times. He came within sight of
the cottage. It stood above the surrounding water, and the
orchard, on raised ground, had become a haven for a restless
flock of starlings and sparrows. Looking at the birds, he was
reminded of the one that had been with Old Tom the last time
he had seen him. There was no sign of it now. No doubt, after
the death of the man, the bird had been forced to seek food
elsewhere. He glanced up at the sky, wondering if the familiar
shape would be circling overhead, but there was only a
scattering of woodpigeons searching for a field in which to
feed.

He reached the gateway at the end of the path. Extensive
patches of snow still lay in the orchard; elsewhere the ground
was soft and sodden. He walked slowly down the path.

"Underneath the nearest apple tree, he was," his father had
said. "On his back, looking up at the sky with as peaceful a
look on his face as I've seen on any man. It must have been
just like a light going out; on one moment, and off the next."

Geraint stared at the spot. There was nothing but grass,
which had been flattened everywhere by the weight of the
snow. A few metres away, in a hollow between the trees, snow
still lay, melting rapidly.

He went to the house. The door had a padlock on it, put
there by his father. Geraint turned away, his throat tighten-
ing. It was unlikely he would be going into the cottage again.
He wondered what would happen to it now. Probably it
would be sold as a weekend retreat to one of the thousands of
city-dwellers who were buying up every vacant building in the
countryside, including derelict byres. He glanced across the
orchard, at the line of hives standing still and silent, though

he knew they were filled with dormant life waiting like buds to break open in spring sunlight. They would doubtless be removed before long, and taken over by someone in the village. His father had told him that the goat, which had been found thin and half-starved in the pen at the back, had already been taken to Ma Lewis.

As he walked back down the path, he caught sight of something just below the surface of the snow in the orchard. Squelching across the soft ground, he reached the spot and stood, staring down, unbelieving. It was still half buried, but he knew what it was. Stooping, he scraped away the snow with his bare hand and carefully, reverently, lifted up the body of the raven.

The body was unmarked and well preserved by having been frozen. Geraint's tears flowed unashamedly now, for his emotions had been at breaking point before this discovery. He never knew how long he stood there, holding the heavy bird and trying to piece together in his mind how the strange coincidental deaths of man and bird could have occurred.

Blinking away his tears, he crossed to the outhouse where he knew the bird had roosted during its last days. From within, he took a spade and went back to the spot where he had found the bird. There, in the precise place where it had died, he dug down almost a metre deep and into the grave he laid the great, black body. He shovelled back the earth to cover it and from the path near the outhouse he fetched a large piece of slate, one which had fallen from the dilapidated roof. With the tine of a garden fork he scratched the letters: BLACKIE. He went across and placed it on the grave.

The ledge on which the nest was built was sheltered on three sides and even the exceptional winds had done no damage. Even so, Corax and Rega began to add new material to the massive mound of twigs that was the fruit of centuries of raven labour. It rose like a giant cairn, stopping short only a metre or so from the overhang of solid rock. The age-old site had been cleverly selected, for the nest was virtually in an alcove halfway up the sheer west face of Craig-y-Cigfran. The half-hearted nest-building being carried out by the two ravens was a courtship ritual, one of many which Corax would instinctively be performing in his efforts to woo and win Rega as his mate.

The first demonstration of affection took place in the air the day following their first night of roosting on the ledge. For the whole of that day, Corax indulged in aerobatics. While Rega soared nonchalantly above the peaks, Corax would rise high above her and nose-dive past her with closed wings, opening them in time to skim the rocks and soar again, sometimes somersaulting, before again flying strongly past her, turning and twisting in a corkscrew roll before tumbling as though out of control. At times, flying on his back, he would hurtle past her upside-down, then corkscrew to normal flight and plummet like a falcon on an imaginary prey. After such a demonstration, which could last for over an hour, both birds would wing back to the nest. There, on the ledge beside it, Corax continued his courtship with a display.

First, he stood apart from her, lifting and lowering his head while at the same time raising the tufts of feathers above and behind his eyes. Then he walked towards her until he was beside her and, uttering a medley of nasal sounds and clacking with his bill, he stretched his long neck above hers. With his head and neck feathers and the large throat feathers spread out like a ruff, he bowed continuously while keeping up the chattering, popping, rasping trill. Next, he sank down on his belly, stretching his neck out with his beak pointing downwards and stayed in this position to the accompaniment of a repeated chorus of curious gutteral grating and clacking sounds.

The demonstrative song and dance, performed by Corax for the first time in his life with instinctive mastery of every note and step, had an immediate effect. Rega, who had stood subdued and attentive, stretched out and began to preen his out-thrust neck feathers. He made a similar move and the two indulged in mutual preening for several minutes. This stimulated Corax to leap into the air which, within the confines of the ledge, led to him buffeting against the overhang. Undeterred, he did this several times, landing finally beside Rega.

The female raven stood motionless. Opening his great bill, Corax took her beak into his and stroked it, releasing it and ruffling her under the chin, for all the world like a demonstrative kiss. He repeated this bill-stroking, kissing ritual until it was Rega's turn to jump up and down. She repeated this until finally she prostrated herself with her belly to the rock and Corax mounted her.

That first brief union at their nest site signified their union for life. As if in celebration, the two birds took off from the mountainside and soared higher than they had ever been before. There, above the crags, in the wintry haze of the January sky, their ecstatic nuptial flight seemed to manifest the spirit of the very element that had created and shaped them; aerial forms which could conquer the winds and lift themselves free from the earthly world. Higher and higher they flew, then plummeted, rolling and twisting, to skim the topmost peaks as though contemptuous of their immobility. The harsh calls echoed across the misty silence of the valley as Corax, with his mate beside him, celebrated the fulfilment of his existence.

14. Spring

Although there was no further snow, the cold persisted into February. But for all the notice that Corax and Rega took, it might as well have been spring. These were carefree days for both birds. Between their frequent couplings, they continued their nuptial flights, ranging great distances without feeling the need to hunt or scavenge, pursuing each other along the mountain passes with Corax uttering a vibrating call quite unlike his usual croaking bark and following Rega to the nest where, standing close beside her, he would caress her bill with his until she raised her head, then tickle her below the chin before hopping to one side and picking up a twig, presenting it to her with a courtly bowing motion. Sometimes, he would fly and return with a pebble as a gift, nudging her until she took it from him in her bill. At other times, he would pull her tail in play, or, when offering her a twig, jerk it away just as she was about to take it. His courtship antics seemed to know no bounds. Once, he held a pebble in his feet while on the ledge and toppled over until he lay on his back with the pebble still clasped in his outstretched claws.

Soon, however, the behaviour of the pair became more

purposeful. They began to bring back more twigs and added yet one more layer to the already towering nest. Next, they returned with heather stalks and moss which they mixed with mud carried in their beaks to form a bowl-shape. This they lined with grass and hair and with the wool that they plucked from the tufts snagged on the wire fences of the farms.

On the third day of February, Rega laid her first egg, pear-shaped and bluish-green blotched with black and brown. That night, while Rega was sitting on it, Corax roosted on the ledge. But Rega was not brooding. She flew to feed next day, returned and laid a second egg. Each day for three more days, she laid an egg until the clutch of five was complete. On the fifth day, after an early morning feed, she returned and settled down to incubate in earnest.

Only Rega did the brooding. Corax had the task of feeding her and this he did with devoted regularity. All the food he brought was carrion, for on the farms the lambing had begun with all its aftermath and stillborn animals. With swollen food-pouch, he would fly towards the ledge, greeting her with a barking *korronk, korronk* as he came within sight. When he landed, his call softened to a chattering *pruk, pruk, pruk* while Rega, peering from the nest, welcomed him with a high-pitched, querulous squawk and fluffed up her feathers as she sat waiting to be fed. Hopping up to her, Corax deposited the contents of his pouch. Sometimes, he would stay to watch her feed, even helping her by picking up morsels and letting her take them from his beak, all the while maintaining the bubbling, rasping chatter. Once his pouch was empty, he would stay preening his feathers for a while before setting off on another flight of several miles to refill his pouch and return to repeat the procedure.

There were occasions when his foraging took second place. An unwanted visitor would venture too near the nest. Often, they were unsuspecting jackdaws, now beginning to look for nest sites. Their searches were abruptly terminated by the hurtling form of Corax as he appeared from nowhere, almost before his loud warning calls had been heard. Buffeted and frightened, the jackdaws fled, pursued by Corax until they were beyond the territory that the raven regarded as his.

Other visitors were less easily put to flight. A visiting male raven met the first onslaught of Corax with almost equal aggression. Corax, surprised at first, recovered from the counter-attack and, having the greater incentive of a mate and eggs to defend, pursued the attack with more vigour than the bird seeking a nest-site could command. After several minutes of aerial combat, when claw and bill sent puffs of black down and feathers scattering in the wind, he succeeded in putting the intruder to flight.

He fared less well with a peewit flock whose feeding in a valley field he interrupted. The vigilant cock sentinel rose at his approach and attacked with such fierceness that Corax was forced to turn tail. But this was not enough, for the whole flock of more than a score of birds, all screaming with anger, chased him far from the field, following him to the crags, and only by seeking cover in a rock fissure did he escape their buffeting and mid-air aggression.

For twenty days Rega sat, keeping the life beneath her at a warm and constant temperature in spite of the fluctuating weather conditions. On the twentieth day, as Corax returned from his first foraging flight, a new sound greeted him from the nest. He flew up and perched beside Rega. The sound was repeated, from beneath the sitting hen. Rega shifted her body and, arching her neck, picked up the broken eggshell, revealing the moist, pink-skinned, bulbous-headed chick which, even as they watched, opened its top-heavy beak and uttered again the cry which of all sounds meant the most to both ravens: the cry of Life.

The remaining four eggs hatched that same day. Before

nightfall, in the late February dusk, Rega went on her first flight for three weeks, stretching her great wings and soaring above Craig-y-Cigfran, while far below her five young felt for the first time the mountain air on their bodies and sent out their shrill, agitated calls for food. The calls held the flighting raven to the mountain like an invisible thread and it was not long before Rega responded, knowing instinctively that her chicks should not be left long without her body's warmth to protect them. Gliding down, she landed at the nest-side and, ignoring their persistent pleas for food, shuffled herself gently in position over them. Darkness found the raven family silent and content.

It was Corax who brought his young their first meal. He left his ledge roost at first light and an hour later he was back with a pouch so crammed with putrid lamb and other carrion that he could not call out a greeting, only a stifled gargling croak as he landed heavily on the nest's edge and disgorged.

Within the nest, which Rega had vacated, it was as though a bunch of vivid flowers had suddenly come into bloom, for the yawning maws of the chicks revealed bright mauve interiors and yellow gapes. Into these, one by one, Corax fed morsels of the food, his great bill dropping them with gentle and careful precision. No sooner had he fed them all the food than Rega, throat-pouch swollen, landed beside him. Stroking her bill with his in a demonstration of affection, he flew up as she continued with the feeding of the young and set out again across the valley.

The five chicks grew rapidly, giving Corax and Rega no respite in the constant search for food. On the valley farms, the lambs had all dropped by the middle of March, so the ravens had to find food by flying further afield. On the marshy flats around Llyn Hewel, Corax found the eggs of redshanks. Past experience had taught him to inspect the stagnant ponds and ditches, and in this way he found the pools to which the frogs had made their annual migrations. Ranging even further, to the coast, both he and Rega were able to vary the diet of the chicks by the inclusion of fish carrion and molluscs.

The young ravens altered visibly as each day passed. The grotesque, naked chicks that had emerged from the eggs soon revealed themselves as clad in mouse-brown down which thickened into downy feathers along the wings and spine and thighs and above their dove-grey eyes. Their enormous stomachs and huge maws became less disproportionate as they grew, and at three weeks old their identity as young ravens was more distinct.

As the fledgelings' size increased, so did their appetites. The two adult birds had little rest and only occasionally, when they paused at midday, could one or other of them indulge in the exuberant aerial demonstrations at which they excelled.

110

It was during such an aerobatic flight by Corax, when the young were four weeks old, that two figures, those of a young man and a girl, appeared walking up the path among the rocks which led from the valley road below. Corax was not perturbed, for the sight of people on the valley side was commonplace and he paid no heed to the two upturned faces as he soared above the peaks, spiralling slowly before suddenly closing his wings and plummeting earthwards past the nest and down, to stall and rise a wing-breadth from the rocks below. Up, up he soared again, above the staring couple, and swept into a somersault before plunging, corkscrewing as he fell, past his young and his watching mate, whose harsh call of greeting carried to him on the mountain wind.

On the path which led up from the valley, Geraint stood, clasping the hand of the girl beside him, gazing up in awe-struck silence. He had watched the aerial displays of ravens many times before, but never had he witnessed such a demonstration of aerobatic skill and mastery. He could tell that Moira, too, appreciated the spectacle, for she was standing, pressed against his side, holding her breath in wonderment.

It had been a spur-of-the-moment decision, this, to walk to Craig-y-Cigfran. For late March, the afternoon had blossomed with the suddenly fulfilled promise of spring and the sun, though low above the peaks, bore the first real warmth of the year. After the sadness of the bitter winter, the sun came doubly welcome to Geraint. The twin deaths of Old Tom and the raven, and the funeral of the old man, which he had attended, had touched his heart with winter frost, leaving a heavy, frozen coldness there. The sun's warmth, mingled as it was with bird song, seemed the only natural cure and was

111

already beginning to melt the ice he still carried within him.

For many weeks now, Geraint had seen no sign of any raven, not since he had buried Blackie in the orchard grave. The thought had suddenly come to him to check if ravens were nesting again at their age-old site. On suggesting it to Moira, she had willingly agreed, for since keeping company with Geraint in recent weeks she had heard all about the ravens and the part they had played in Geraint's life during the past years. In fact, she could herself remember Geraint's young pet bird, Corbie, on its now legendary bus-journeys to and from the school where she had been a fellow-pupil with Geraint.

The two stood watching Corax as his joyful flight continued.

"I wonder if that's Corbie," Geraint said. "The nest on the ledge up there is where he came from and I found him just over here. It could be him, grown up and come back to start his own family."

"He'll have a mate then, won't he?" said the girl, squeezing his hand. "He must have, to be showing off like that."

Geraint saw her teasing smile and laughed, returning her hand's pressure.

"She's probably up there at the nest right now," he said. "Pretending not to be impressed. But she is really, or else she would not be there, see, keeping company with him."

It was the girl's turn to laugh. Geraint continued.

"As like as not, she's up there sitting on eggs, or even young."

The girl pointed as the raven dived towards them. It came low, curious without aggression, before swooping up above their heads and heading back towards the ledge. They saw it prepare to land and Geraint marked the spot with care. It was not far short of a hundred metres above the bank of scree on which they were standing and at first glance looked inac-

112

cessible, but on studying the rockface, Geraint was not so sure. When they finally turned and headed slowly, arm in arm, back down towards the village, Geraint was unusually thoughtful.

15. Discovery

The seed of the idea that had struck Geraint at Craig-y-Cigfran grew and blossomed during the following week. He mentioned it to no one but by asking a few of the villagers and by checking natural history books he established that ravens regularly laid their eggs sometime in February. Since the eggs took three weeks to hatch and the young stayed in the nest a further six, Geraint felt certain that, as it was now early April, the young within the nest at Craig-y-Cigfran would be almost fully fledged. They would be ready to leave the nest at any time now.

When Saturday broke fine and fair, he knew it would be now or never. Mentioning nothing to his mother of his intentions, he left after breakfast as though going to call for Moira as he usually did.

He walked along the valley road, preoccupied with his thoughts. The sun was already lighting the western face of Craig-y-Cigfran and the gorse flared golden among the rocks below the scree. It took him half an hour to reach the path up to the mountain and he stopped and eyed the towering peak with some misgiving. It was not as if he fully understood his

own reasons for coming. Certainly it was something to do
with Old Tom and his Blackie; and it also had to do with
Corbie, and whether or not the bird now nesting at the site of
Corbie's birth was the same bird, returned. Perhaps there was
no single reason for the urge he felt, perhaps it was the sum of
all these, and more besides. Perhaps it was a tribute to Old
Tom, to emulate the man's own boyhood climb up to the
ledge on Foel Ddu, long since collapsed in an avalanche of
dust and crumbled rock. He could not even say it was the
passionate desire to possess another raven, though that was
certainly his intention. That, too, could be another emulation
of Old Tom.

No clearer about his motives than before, Geraint followed
the steep path made by the hardy sheep up to the mountain
face. As he neared it, he heard the cry, the hollow, echoing
croak that never failed to stir him, and as the harsh sound
rebounded from the black rocks, it seemed to be the strongest
motive of all: he was responding to the raven's call.

The sound persisted as he continued up the path. Then the
bird came into view, lifting from the ledge above and moving
out over him, the great jagged wings outstretched as it slowly
spiralled down.

Geraint wondered if it would attack him, and waved his
arms. The bird veered off, alarmed, and the croak became a
succession of angry barks. He remembered his last encounter
with an adult raven defending its young, almost at this very
spot, and also Old Tom's story of being attacked, and when
the bird began to descend again, he shouted as well as waved.
Again, the bird sheered away.

"Let's hope you do not get any braver than that," thought
Geraint, as he reached the final bend of the track.

Twenty metres or so from the foot of the mountain,
Geraint halted and studied the face. Now he was closer, he
could see several places to begin the climb, but he knew from

115

past experience that it did not always pay to take the easiest start. He knew the position of the ledge by the jutting brow of the overhang above it, and letting his eye travel down from that point, he picked a route that seemed to offer the best holds. To get to that line, he would have to reach the top of a small smooth slab of granite that stood some eight metres high just to his left. He quickly located the best route to the top of that and, bracing himself, moved towards it.

His head for heights was good and like all the other boys from the village who had roamed the valley slopes from their earliest years, rock climbing had become second nature to him. He zipped his anorak up to his neck, took off his wristwatch and put it into his pocket, and making sure his shoelaces were properly tied, for a loose lace had once given him a foot-slipping scare, he began the ascent to the persistent *pruk, pruking* of the circling raven.

The first stage was difficult because the rock was so smooth, but once he had reached the top of the slab, the going was easier. He climbed carefully, without haste, testing each handhold and foothold before putting his whole weight on it. He estimated the distance to the ledge at between sixty and seventy metres and he had covered twenty of these before the climb became really taxing.

The trouble was the angle. The rock below the ledge in many places bulged from the otherwise sheer face and although he could see plenty of holds, it was clear his body would be forced outwards at certain points. He stayed motionless, secure in a good position, and studied the rock ahead. From now on, every move must be planned. The raven's cries were becoming more agitated and, turning his head slowly, he saw that there were two, circling near the ledge and voicing a tirade of staccato, grating protests. Praying that they would not actually attack him, Geraint moved his hand up to the next hold.

The going was slow. At one point, his right leg, stretched and tense, began to tremble and he had no alternative but to lower himself to rest the tautened nerve. But he persevered and the rock-bulges were not as formidable as they had appeared from below. There was one moment when his heart stopped; one of the ravens appeared to have made up its mind to attack. It flew closer to his head than ever, uttering a warning *korronk* that resounded in his ear. But at the last moment it veered away and Geraint felt the rush of air and heard the singing of the bird's feathers as it passed. For some reason, it did not repeat the tactic, and from then on his progress was uneventful, though not for one second did he relax his care. When his hands grasped the edge of the actual ledge, he ached in every limb and his breath was rasping in his chest. He hauled himself on to the ledge and lay there, as happy at that moment as he could ever remember being.

A short respite was all he needed, however, and he sat up and took stock of his surroundings. At first, he did not recognise the nest. The ledge, some five metres long and three or four deep, looked bare except for the wall of twigs at one end. Only when he stood up did he realise that this mound, which was as tall as he was, was the nest. Once upright, he could see the top of it and the second realisation struck him. The noise he could hear, a continuous, unrelieved, monotonous squawk, like a strident buzz-saw, was the concert of pleas from the purple-mawed young he could see in the nest-top depression, their gaping beaks jutting up like a cluster of blossoming snapdragons. This cacophony was augmented from behind him as the two circling ravens added their harsh complaints.

But it was not only the noise that brought home to Geraint the bizarreness of his situation. There was the stench; the accumulated scraps of old putrefying flesh lay thick around the nest, some on the ledge, some lodged on the twigs, and all attracting flies and other insects. It was so unexpected, so unlike anything he had imagined, that his sense of humour pricked him to a smile. To have risked his life climbing seventy metres up a sheer granite mountain to end up surrounded by flies and rotten meat, screeching ravens and the largest nest he had ever seen had an incongruity which appealed to him. He almost laughed aloud but then, as he glanced round, the sight that met his eyes took away all thoughts of the bizarre.

It was the most breathtaking view he had ever seen of the valley. He had never climbed so high before and the whole sweep stretched out below him. He could see the mountains at the far end curving round as they made way for the river, and the blunt escarpment of Esgair Fawr beyond Foel Ddu formed a giant wall below which lay the miniature farms and wall-divided cattle-dotted fields. Across these were the winding scars of sheep-tracks with the countless grey puffs of sheep specking the green like dandelion seeds. Down the valley centre went the glinting road with a desultory stream of vehicles moving slowly up and down. On the distant knoll, which he knew must be at least three miles off, the tall Scots pines stood marking the pass through the peaks followed by the ancient drovers' road which led past Dinas Bran. Geraint gazed and understood the real meaning of a bird's-eye view. He knew now why generation after generation of ravens had chosen the site. Any bird that nested here commanded the whole valley.

He tore his gaze away, for he had other things to do. Unzipping his anorak, he took out a folded plastic bag and opened it. Ignoring the raucous, agitated cries of the wheeling adult birds, he moved towards the nest, eyeing it apprehensively. It was so high he would have to reach up and grab the nearest fledgeling. He could see that the timing of his visit had been well judged, for the young birds' shoulders were well clad with fully formed feathers. Clearly, it would not be long before they left the nest.

He moved forward and paused. For some reason, it suddenly seemed wrong, to do what he was about to do. But he had come all this way, and at some risk to life and limb, and he shrugged off the feeling and took another cautious step.

His foot scuffed the granite chippings and a faint, metallic ring made him look down. Stooping, he picked up a small metal disc, perhaps a buckle of some kind, for though blackened and corroded with age, it appeared to have a bar or pin across the back of it. As he straightened up, wrinkling his nose in distaste at the smell from the nest, he caught sight of a second object, in among the twigs. Holding his breath, he reached in and retrieved it. This one was a coin, about the size of a two-pence piece, also blackened with age. Brushing off the dust and the dirt, he found he could just discern the imprint of several letters: ___ERUS IMP on one side around the impression of a head; and on the other side:

_ _ _ORIAE_ _ IT. These, he knew, were parts of Latin words and his heart quickened as he realised the coin might even be a Roman one. Putting both objects carefully into his pocket, he knelt down and, regardless now of the stench, began to examine the foundations of the massive nest more carefully.

The task was difficult as well as dirty. The ancient branches and twigs snapped and turned to powder as he touched them and the accumulated dirt, moss, bird-droppings and detritus of centuries soon covered him. But his excitement became intense as he made more finds. Crouched on his knees with his head and shoulders thrust into the stack, he was unable to examine them but thrust the objects deep into his pocket. A length of metal, tarnished with age, was lodged in the twigs and he tugged it free, breaking the wood in a puff of dust that made him sneeze. Another small metal object, too thick for a coin, and a second flat disc of reddish metal, perforated by small holes, went into his pocket. Before long, he had made a virtual tunnel through the base of the stack and the whole structure was in danger of collapsing, bringing the nestlings with it. Satisfied that there was nothing else he could reasonably expect to find without destroying the nest, he retreated until he was able to stand upright. Brushing the filth from his hair and clothes, he sat down to examine his finds.

By now, the two adult ravens were showing distress. His presence was preventing them from answering the incessant pleas of the fledgelings. Geraint looked at the wheeling birds, and the plaintiveness in their drawn-out croaking cries had its effect on him.

He repocketed his treasures without identifying any except the coin, but he felt certain that the other objects were equally old. Knowing as he did the ways of ravens, and remembering Corbie's habit of flying off with any glittering object that attracted him, Geraint was sure that the earliest ravens to build on the ledge had brought back their shining treasures, taken from nearby; contemporary objects, such as the coin. This could mean that ravens had been nesting here since Roman times, when the valley below had held the living quarters of the legionnaires, and the ancient fort beside Old Tom's cottage had been occupied. Geraint's imagination raced but the raven's harsh call brought him up short.

He got to his feet, his mind made up. His climb had brought success beyond his wildest hopes and this, together with the evident distress of both the adult and the fledgeling ravens caused him to change his mind about taking a young bird with him. He would leave them, wild and untamed, to enjoy their ancient home and the freedom it signified. Taking a last look at the nest and the panorama of the valley, he approached the edge, turned and lowered himself to the footholds by which he had made his ascent.

The climb down was more of an ordeal than he had anticipated. His first anxiety was the aggressiveness of the two adult ravens. Seeing him spreadeagled against the rockface, both birds came more dangerously close than before, and several times Geraint was sure he was actually going to be attacked. Each time they swooped at him, he sheltered his face between projecting rocks and they turned aside at the last second, brushing his head with their wings. As he descended, however, the attacks diminished and, to Geraint's relief, he heard the continuous raucous clamour of the nestlings above his head suddenly intensify and then quieten abruptly. Their feeding had been resumed, which signified that he was no longer being regarded as an obstacle. Taking a slow, deep breath to calm himself, he concentrated on his remaining descent.

His recollection of the upward route was good and as he inched his way down, he found he could remember every hold. But the bulge below the ledge was tricky and there was a heart-stopping moment when his foot could not find the hold he knew was there. He had to twist his neck and look down over his shoulder and the sight of the sheer drop of thirty metres directly below him made even his stomach turn. But his exceptional head for heights and his steady nerve and calmness did not desert him and, once he had passed that spot, the rest of the descent was uneventful. By the time he reached the ground, however, his arms and legs were trembling with the effort and as he backed from the rockface he had to fight an inexplicable urge to break into tears.

He sat for fifteen minutes, with his head in his hands, drawing deep breaths and waiting until he felt more in command of his limbs and his emotions. When he eventually stood up, he looked back up at the ledge, and only then did the enormity of the risk he had taken really strike him. He wandered slowly down the path towards the road, marvelling at his own achievement and survival.

He arrived home at lunchtime, shocking his mother by his dirty, dishevelled appearance. She was even more aghast when she learned how he had come to be in such a state. But when, after lunch, he brought out his finds and showed them to his parents, Geraint could tell at once they were beginning to share his pride in the achievement.

The objects were difficult, if not impossible, to identify and both Geraint and his father knew it was important not to clean them too vigorously. But after brushing off the worst of the dirt, it appeared that Geraint had returned with a coin; a button of some kind; the object which Geraint thought could be some kind of buckle; and two quite unidentifiable metal items, one in the form of a thin strip and the other flat and perforated and which could be almost anything.

Geraint's father, growing more enthusiastic by the minute, suggested what should be the next step. He had a friend in Llanfair, David Pugh, who was a keen archaeologist. He would know what to do with the finds. Mr Rees stood up and crossed to the telephone.

122

Early that evening, taking Moira with him, Geraint caught the bus to Llanfair and spent a pleasant hour with the archaeologist describing how he had made the discoveries. The man was impressed, beyond doubt, and Geraint sensed from his attitude that the finds might be even more important than he had realised. He willingly left them to be expertly cleaned and identified. By the time he and Moira returned to Carfan, the story of his climb had reached the Carfan Arms and in the noisy, crowded bar, Geraint was given a folk-hero's welcome; a recognition which, for the rest of the evening, he enjoyed to the full.

16. The Gift

The distress caused by the visit of the human intruder soon disappeared. Corax had been as aggressive as Rega in defence of the nest, for although his relationship with humans when he was young had created an affinity at the time, he had no way of knowing that the intruder had been none other than the boy who had raised him. Since then, of course, his experience of life had diminished the bond. What little remained was now totally subdued and governed by the overwhelming, instinctive need to protect his young. His attitude to the visitor, therefore, had been that of any other wild raven. Like Rega, he had gone for the head of the descending climber with real aggression and only the obstacles of the protruding rock had prevented his beak and claws from inflicting damage.

Corax had, however, been the first to abandon the attacks and resume the feeding of the clamouring young. Picking up one of the half-gorged rat carcasses from the base of the nest, he tore it into shreds and fed the frenzied nestlings. Rega soon came to join him in the task and the retreating intruder was forgotten.

Coping with the young birds' demand for food was the constant occupation of both the parents. Raven chicks stay longer in the nest than the young of any of the crow kind and not until the end of the sixth week were the five nestlings fully fledged and ready to leave the nest. During all this time, Corax and Rega were undergoing their moult. As always, once the primaries had dropped and before new feathers had grown to replace them, their powers of flight were not at their best. Consequently, after forty days of strenuous attention to their young, both adults were looking the worse for wear. It was time for them to act with instinctive ruthlessness in order to help both young and old survive.

During their seventh week of life, the five chicks, now fully fledged, suddenly found themselves at midday calling in vain for food. Corax and Rega had departed from the nest-site and had flown the valley's length to the Scots pines that had often provided them with a resting place. Having fed well in the nearby farm fields, they indulged their new-found freedom by planing in wide circles on the air currents before settling in the trees to roost. This apparent desertion served a twofold purpose: it would give the exhausted and bedraggled moulting birds a chance to rest and to recuperate; and with their parental obligations devotedly carried out, it would oblige their fledgelings to find their wings and fight for their own survival.

And this they did, with one exception. The next day, hungry and complaining loudly, all five fluttered from the nest down to the ledge. There, they found the putrid flesh of meals which Corax and Rega had disgorged or which had toppled from the nest. For one more day they stayed, stretching and flapping their wings, roosting on the ledge, even warning off a predatory herring gull which abruptly abandoned its hope of a meal on finding itself facing a raucous chorus of protests and five huge, threatening bills.

Next morning, soon after dawn, the birds took off one by one, flying clumsily to other ledges or descending to the rocks protruding from the scree below. The last bird lifted off but a sudden gust of wind took it further than the others, out above the valley road. The fledgeling's flight, though laboured, was strong enough to carry it and it headed confidently for the nearest convenient place to perch: the tall pylon that reared from the roadside field and which carried the electric power to Carfan through its lines. The buzzing of the insulators sent out an unheeded warning and the bird struck the wires, dying in a burning instant and dropping, flutter-feathered, charred and smouldering to the earth below. Above it, on the scree-clad slopes, the four other young ravens made increasing flights before setting out on their first forage for food.

Corax and Rega roosted in the pines for two more weeks before returning to the nest-site. They found it empty and deserted save for a stock dove which had laid a pair of milk-white eggs in a desultory nest of twigs below the ravens' own nest. Corax chased the sitting hen away and returned to find Rega finishing the second egg, her bill yellow with yolk. He took her bill in his, stroking it, croaking softly as he did so. Then both birds flew together over the valley, *pruk, pruking* as they went.

The frequent mists and rain of spring softened the valley, preparing it for the lush burgeoning of summer. Bracken fronds spread over the stark slopes of scree so that the mountains appeared to rise from a gently undulating green sea. Ferns fringed the tops of the dry-stone walls, thrusting from the gaps between the thick slate slabs. Young frisking lambs grew plump and more sedate. On the bracken-shaded slopes, life abounded beneath the green canopy. By day, voles, mice and shrews sought to survive the stooping peregrine and pouncing kestrel; and by night, the silent fanning owls or darting weasel, stoat and fox. On the farms, rats multiplied but were kept down by predators which included Corax and his mate. The increased rabbit population, too, provided the raven pair with easy pickings as the continuing cycle of life revolved in the summer-clad valley and mountains as it had for thousands of years.

The advancing season brought a natural change in Carfan, too. Geraint, now approaching his eighteenth year, became more and more inseparable from Moira. When their school work allowed, their walks would take them to the quiet places of the countryside where it was so easy to imagine they were the only two left in the world.

It was towards the end of May when Geraint, meeting Moira in the afternoon, suggested that they walk to Craig-y-Cigfran. Not since his epic climb six weeks before had he been so far up the valley and Moira fell in at once with his desire to revisit the spot. But he had another purpose, one which he did not tell her.

Nestling in his pocket was a brooch that was well over a thousand years old.

The previous day, his finds had been returned to him by David Pugh, who had called at his home unexpectedly. As he had given them back to Geraint, beginning with the brooch, the archaeologist had described their probable history. He had begun by laying down the brooch on the table.

"This is a brooch-clasp, Geraint, made in the third or fourth century. It was used to pin a cloak and was most likely worn on the shoulder. It is bronze and those small decorative designs show it was made by a Celt, though that does not necessarily mean that it was worn by a Celt. These were made in large numbers by the native tribes for trading with the Romans so I expect this was worn by a Roman. As it is quite ornate, this one was most likely for a woman."

"Is it valuable?" Geraint had asked, barely able to contain his surprised excitement.

"Not especially. There were so many of them, you see. Most museums have some. But it's a lovely memento for you to keep, Geraint. As for your other finds, I'm hoping you'll agree to let the museum have them."

He had then produced the coin, now cleaned and with the imprinting on it clearly identifiable.

"This is Roman, too, and you did well not to try scraping the dirt off. We cleaned it in a laboratory tank using a special process called electro-chemical reduction. As you can see, it has come out beautifully. It's a silver denarius minted during the reign of Septimus Severus at the end of the second century. See the inscription."

Geraint recognised some of the letters.

"You see that IMP there? That stands for *Imperator* meaning Emperor. And on the back are the words *Victoriae Brit*. The winged lady is Victory with a captive. Not a rare coin but a nice specimen."

He paused and gave Geraint a third object. This had been unrecognisable when he had found it. Now he could see it was a flat piece of bronze or copper stamped out in a wing-like scroll-shape and perforated by five holes.

"It is a bronze cuirass hinge, Geraint. Late Roman, fourth century probably. The cuirass was metal body armour worn by all fighting legionnaires and this linked the breastplate with the back piece. A most interesting find."

The archaeologist then put down on the table the long metal strip Geraint had extracted from the tangled branches of the nest.

"This one is a piece of brass shield-binding from a Saxon warrior's shield, sixth or seventh century, I would say. And your last object is even later."

128

He gave it to Geraint. It was a button with a pattern
embossed on it.

"It's a silver button from the uniform of a soldier serving
under King James the First, in the early part of the
seventeenth century. Almost certainly the silver came from
the Welsh mines. You can see the Prince of Wales plumes
embossed there. I will leave you to imagine how a raven came
by all these military pieces but they were known to gather
over battlefields, weren't they?"

The man, his task done, had sat back, looking pleased. "A
fascinating collection, Geraint, and, as I say, there is a
museum already interested in negotiating with you. I con-
gratulate you, boy."

Geraint, who had listened to the description of his finds
with a mounting feeling of awe, had found little to say. To
think that all these objects had come from a raven's nest. He
marvelled at the span of history the successive generations of
birds nesting at the site had covered, their pickings linking the
centuries in a way that made the distant past seem like
yesterday.

He had left all the items with the archaeologist except the
bronze clasp; he had something special in mind for that,
which was why he had it with him now as he set out with
Moira along the valley road.

The afternoon sun was high above the village as they left,
her arm through his. They branched off over the bridge and
took the winding path up the slope towards the towering
mountain of Craig-y-Cigfran. The usually sombre granite
was touched by the sunlight into a multitude of shades: green
tufts of bracken; patches of orange and red lichen; clumps
of yellow gorse and the white and russet veins of the rock
itself.

They stopped a hundred metres from the foot of the
mountain and sat among the ferns. From there, Geraint

could see the black mouth of the nest-site yawning far above them.

Moira studied the spot and shook her head in disbelief.

"I had forgotten how high it was. I don't know how you did it, Geraint."

"Nor do I," said Geraint, truthfully.

They lay back, looking at the sky. Within seconds, a raven had appeared from nowhere. Watching it in silence as the great bird spiralled down, Geraint marvelled at the slow, majestic flight. The bird was like no other and, silhouetted against the sky, with the peak of Craig-y-Cigfran behind, it was as much a part of the valley as the mountain itself.

Which in truth it was, Geraint reflected; for had not mountain and bird shared a past older than that of Man? Ravens had been here to see Man's coming. They had watched the early dwellers in the caves and soared above the first paths worn through the forests and the passes. They had seen the arrival of the Celts and the centuries of tribal wars; the clashes with the Romans; the medieval castles rise from the stones; the farms divide the land; the driving of the cattle along roads following those early tracks, roads which Geraint himself still walked. And throughout this long acquaintance the bird had played a significant role, becoming part of men's superstitions.

Geraint smiled to himself. The raven's curious hold on the imagination had not yet disappeared. He felt it still, and he knew Old Tom had, too. It was nothing he could define, or even talk about. But it was there, like an invisible thread, linking him with Old Tom and with the ancient earthwork of the fort and with the mountain, and it all stemmed from the bird that soared above him now, there in the wind, circling black, leaf-winged, all-seeing, high above his head. But no! Not high, but low and close, for the bird stooped suddenly and landed on a rock not thirty metres distant.

Geraint sat up and Moira followed suit. Corax, for he it was, stared a moment, flew further off and settled again.

Geraint laughed. "He thought we were dead, see. If we lie down again, he'll come back."

Geraint was right. They lay back and Corax returned to the rock, then to the next and finally down to the ground, hopping obliquely until he was only a few metres from the motionless prostrate figures.

They sat up and the bird was off, beating the air and rising to the height of the ledge. From the shadow came a second raven and the two birds circled, calling harshly.

Geraint felt in his pocket and brought out the brooch. Moira sat wide-eyed, saying nothing.

"A gift from the ravens, Moira," he said, as he pinned it to her blouse. "Sixteen hundred years it is since this was pinned to a girl's dress by a young man."

Moira looked down at the glinting bronze and the delicate decorative motif.

"It is the most beautiful thing I have ever seen," she breathed. "I will treasure it always."

Above the couple the raven pair chased each other across the valley, spiralling and tumbling, twisting and turning in an exuberant display of affection. Higher and higher they went until the couple below could see only specks in the sky.

Down, down came the birds, then up, between the jagged crags of Craig-y-Cigfran, now in the sun, now lost in the shade, and the harsh, drawn-out croak resounded through the gaps so that it was difficult to tell from where the cry came: from the soaring, shadow-black birds; or from the timeless rocks themselves.

FOX

Flik, a dog fox born on a South Midlands Farm, is the hero of this book. He arouses mixed feelings wherever he goes. He is at once befriended and persecuted, hated and admired. While his story is fictional, all the details are based on fact. It is a fascinating and moving story, full of insights into a fox's way of life. The story is accompanied by 40 evocative illustrations by William Finch.

This is what the critics said:

Scrupulous accurate description of an animal in its natural setting. An unsentimental, detailed and absorbing view of a fox who is never humanised. A fine story.

GROWING POINT

Glyn Frewer does a remarkably persuasive job of explaining the ways of foxes and the ambivalence of mankind towards them.

SUNDAY TIMES

Excellent animal story, neither comic nor sad, but an entertainingly written life-cycle of a fox.

DAILY MAIL

The tale is as much about the countryside as about the chief characters. The author's account of the great hunt intended to dispose of Flik once and for all is a small masterpiece of organisation and animal logic.

THE JUNIOR BOOKSHELF

A story with a fresh country feel to it, an adventure novel about a family of foxes – presented partly as an authentic documentary of the foxes' way of life, food, preferences and habitat while also being an exciting narrative of fox versus man.

GOOD HOUSEKEEPING